ARACHNAPOCALYPSE! THE ANTHOLOGY

ARACHNAPOCALYPSE! UNIVERSE

JB LETTERCAST JUSTIN M. SLOAN CW HAWES
MARÍA G. ORELLANA

All situations and characters herein are original works of fiction.

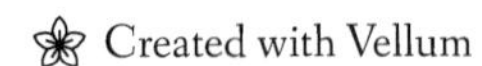

CONTENTS

To my young self and to anyone with a story inside them waiting to see the light of day. Write what you love. Damn the naysayers.

FOREWORD

My name is JB Lettercast. *Arachnapocalypse! The Anthology* is my debut project, my literary baby. The creation of this universe came about in the winter of 2020. The pandemic was still in its early stages, and I had not written anything seriously in several months. As I began my work on a little one-shot story titled *Violet Winter*, I found that my writer's block was starting to melt. As it turns out, I was using the creative process to begin coping with everything that changed in my life that year, as I'm sure you'll see in my work.

As these things sometimes do, the *Arachnapocalypse!* Universe turned into more than just a therapy piece. The further I went into the story, the more there was to reveal through my writing, and the more I had to get out on paper. Over the next year, more stories in this universe revealed themselves to me, and a timeline began to form. At first, I was going to publish a collection of four short stories titled *Arachnapocalypse!* toward the end of 2021.

But then an idea came to me. I really liked the thought of other people playing around in this little world I built. I reached out to some other authors and invited them to work on the project with me, with a goal publication date of October 2022. I couldn't offer them much, not even royalties. But the concept was exciting enough that I got a few takers, and we set to work getting the timeline fleshed out through the art of short-story-telling.

The stories in *Arachnapocalypse! the Anthology* offer glimpses into the end of the world as we knew it, and the dawn of a new and violent age. Each story centers around different characters, at different times and locations, all between the arrival of the Arachnids in late 2018 and the raid on the Mars outpost in the distant future. The universe and storytelling styles are very extra – and they're meant to be! The themes here are inspired by the likes of Warhammer, Star Trek, Event Horizon, The Walking Dead, and Starship Troopers.

There's love and war, kindness and deception, and a whole lot of bugs.

As authors and creatives, our goal is to provide the reader with captivating worlds that walk the line between fantastical and honest. We strive to give you a place to escape, but also to make you *feel something*. It is our imperative to draw attention to the human condition and shine a light on the complexities and contradictions that come with being a person – all without taking ourselves too seriously. I hope these stories do that for you. If anything, I hope to give you an enjoyable afternoon away from whatever is happening in your life.

Sincerely,

JB Lettercast

ABOUT THE AUTHORS

CW Hawes

Hawes is a multi-genre author and award-winning poet. He is the author of over 20 post-apocalyptic, mystery, alternative history, and horror novels and stories.

JB Lettercast

JB Lettercast is a queer, multi-genre author and poet with a passion for dark, gritty, speculative fiction. He got his start writing nonfiction children's books for Teacher Created Materials in 2011. He is spearheading the VeryGood Collab Books yearly author collaboration project.

María Gabriela Orellana

Orellana is an Argentinian STEM major and freelance author. She loves gothic fiction, historical fiction, poetry, medieval fantasy, and RPGs.

Justin M. Sloan

Sloan is a video game writer, novelist, and screenwriter. He studied writing at the Johns Hopkins University and screenwriting the UCLA School of Theater, Film and Television. He served in the U.S. Marines for five years.

Merlin Spoke

Spoke is an award-winning flash-fiction author, Warhammer enthusiast, and active duty service member.

VeryGood Collab Books

We want to feature you in our next anthology! Apply to write in our yearly author collaboration project at verygoodcollab.com!

1

VIOLET WINTER

JB LETTERCAST

Crisp snow sat in silent reverence against a commanding blue sky. The high sun made crystals of melting snow sparkle on the foothill horizon. The wind was barely a whisper across the coulee. Squads of guardian trees towered over the sleepy landscape, ever watchful. Face red and fingers stiff, Sue had battled against biology all day to maintain a steady aim. So far, she had caught nothing. The shivering of her calorie-starved body made for sloppy shots at the small, dancing targets of ptarmigan and rabbit. The distant sun's warmth was no match for the swell of cold emanating from the earth. Sore fingers notched an arrow. She could feel time and stamina running out on her. At this rate, her journey back to the burrow would take her into the dangerous gray hours of dusk. This shot had to count for something, or she would go home empty-handed once more. She pulled the arrow back hard against the bowstring and fixed her aim, then released a trembling breath and let the arrow fly. The rabbit had no time to react. It dropped to the ground with a squeal, and its surprised companion sprang desperately off into the brush. Finally, Sue would have something more than shrinking rations of fish jerky and old potatoes to eat. Angry fangs of hunger gnawed at her gut. Sue wanted to eat now, but she *needed* to survive the winter. She still had hours of hunting to go.

The trek back to her burrow in the wilderness was not an easy one. The passage was a series of tricky scrambles up and down treacherous rocky passages, each one slick with ice fortified by the evening chill. In the few hours since her first rabbit, she had managed to snag three more, and with four fresh rabbits on her back, Sue's spirits were up. It was a small but crucial reward. Still, she had used up more hunting hours than there were in the day. Now she had to pay the price. Traversing near three miles of cold, rocky terrain in such poor lighting, she ran the risk of injury or even death. Even still, she was safer here than in any of the surrounding cities. As the temperature sank even lower and the waxing gibbous painted the land silver, the forest around her became utterly silent. Any creature that valued its life was hiding deep in the earth by now, huddled up for warmth and on high alert for a sign of the new predators that had arrived last year.

At last, she reached the stream that passed her dwelling. Its icy, dripping trickle was loud against the sheer silence of the forest. Snow had not yet padded the ground in this deep valley. Most of what snow had fallen weighed down the thicket surrounding the place. Sue knew that after a few more weeks, she would spend most of her time inside, waiting out frigid winter storms. But it was hard to think so far ahead, knowing she might not even make it past tonight. Stuttering breath and rattling shivers coming in hard, sharp bursts, she reached the hill where the entrance to her home stood. To her relief, it had remained undisturbed. From the outside, it didn't look like much. It didn't look like much from the inside, either. How could it compare to the home she left to come here? But that simple hole in the ground was everything. Every moment she spent in that darkness was a moment she spent safe and alive.

The entrance, supported by large rocks she'd painstakingly gathered from the river, was well hidden beneath boughs of trees and blankets of moss. Sue liked to believe that anyone who did not know what to look for would not be able to find it. Only time would tell whether or not that was true. Having become intimately acquainted with the landscape here, she always knew what to look for to find her way home. She thanked the near-full moon for lighting her way before going inside. Slipping through the makeshift door, Sue surrendered herself to the darkness. In the beginning months, this place had felt like a tomb. In some ways, it mirrored the style of the burial shafts built by the ancient Egyptians and Toltecs. About three feet into the low entrance was a root cellar. It was five feet deep, covered with a heavy, flat stone to keep animals out. Three feet beyond that was her personal cellar, where she slept six long feet below the surface in a notch she'd built to trap her body heat. She'd spent months digging and building out the burrow as deep as she could get into the ground, as far from the surface of the living world as she could bear to be. It was cold, dark, and musty, but it was safe.

After offloading her kills into the cellar, she climbed down the tangle of old tree roots that served as a ladder into the gravelike shaft where she slept. Wrapped in warm layers of foliage and fabric, nestled into the safety of Mother Earth's arms, Sue resigned herself to sleep. She dreamed of rabbit stew and the warmth of the southern ocean. She dreamed of summer. She dreamed of a big, hot sun. She dreamed of steak and prawns. She dreamed of melting butter on big, fluffy pieces of warm fresh bread. But most of all, Sue dreamed of the time before. She dreamed of a time when humans were not prey, when gathering in groups was not deadly – when most choices were not life and death. Now, as had been the case every day since those damned *things* landed, humans only existed to adapt and overcome. One hardship after another, every precious moment was spent just trying to survive. This year was supposed to be the year she broke free, but instead, she had traded one nightmare for another, only this time, her enemies were numerous and her chances of survival increasingly slim.

Traces of golden sunshine embroidered the otherwise jet-black interior of Sue's earthy abode. The night was over. All around her, the forest had begun to wake and step warily into the light of day. The scent of frosted dew on bristlecone pine wafted down to where she slept. It tangled with her myriad dreams. Even the insects seemed to know it was time to begin their day's work. The tickle of millipede legs in her blankets was Sue's morning alarm now. It was that time of the week when she should lug the nesting up to the surface to shake it out and bathe it in the cleansing sunlight to get rid of the creepy-crawlies that lived there with her. She slowly propped the entrance to the cave open, watching with keen eyes for any sign of predators before stepping out into the open and giving her arms and back a wide stretch. After hanging her blankets out on a limb, she headed down into the food cellar to gather breakfast supplies. It was cold enough here that her buried food remained safe to eat for quite some time. The rabbit carcasses were almost frozen. The cellar was small, but it had enough room for her root vegetables, anything she'd harvested during her hunts, some fresh and dried meat stores, the firewood, and the pot she'd brought with her when she'd fled the south. The sparse space could hardly be called a home, but everything had a use and a place where it belonged.

Since it was impossible to remain hidden with a fire burning constantly, Sue learned how to efficiently start a fire whenever she wanted to eat. Getting a good flame going used up kindling, time, and energy; these three things had characteristically limited quantities. But by now, she was an expert, even in this damp winter climate. Once the fire was going, she started the rabbit stew. Water from the stream, some old potatoes, and a whole cleaned rabbit came together in the pot on the fire. The scent of a hot meal might attract wild predators, but the smoke was her real concern. By now, most of the big game had been consumed by *them*, so the risk of a bear or even a badger running across her camp was slim. *They* hunted based on body heat. The pickings would likely be slim, especially with winter tipping its hand. Every day she survived was a day she came closer to being the last warm body on Earth. She knew that eventually, she would die, and she had made her peace with that. But Sue would rather take her chances with the elements than deliver herself into the jaws of those *beasts*.

The pillar of smoke that rose steadily into the sky and the heat it generated could easily give her position away. Anxiously, she crouched by the flames, stoking them when they needed it and watching the sky and trees. It was hard not to enjoy the warmth emanating from the blaze. Fire had been what made humans special. For eons past, fire had meant life. Now it was the enemy, a death sentence on the tip of the grand judge's tongue. She forced herself to villainize it, so she would not be bereft when she doused or smothered it. As the days grew colder, she had to try even harder to think of it as this deadly thing that could consume and destroy if she let it live. It wouldn't just destroy the forest. Her warm companion bespoke a survivor in the wilderness, telling the tale she wanted desperately to remain untold. It signaled to *them* that she was alive and free for the taking.

At last, the stew was cooked. With a large stick, she removed the pot from the fire, then kicked cold, wet soil over the treacherous tongues of light. Sue brought the pot and her blanket, warmed by sunlight and flame, back into her den to hide for a few hours in case *they* had sent a scout to find the source of the heat. It would be harder for *them* to find her during the day. As the sun crept higher in the sky and heated the ground, her diminishing trace could be interpreted as a patch of sun-heated soil on the forest floor. And even if the scout came down to investigate, she would hear it coming through the canopy, ditch the soup as a deterrent, and hide in her burial shaft. If it found her in there, she would have nowhere to run. But it was a fruitless effort to even consider outrunning Earth's newest apex predators. Still, she had a fighting chance if it entered her home. Sue was never without her dagger. The whole time she'd spent traveling north, many people had tried to barter for it or even steal it from her. But this small weapon she'd purchased at a renaissance faire some years back had proven to be her saving grace on a few occasions.

The dagger was dull when she'd bought it. It was strong, fashioned like a real weapon, but blunted so the vendor could sell it in his stall. Even in the cold dark of her den, if she thought hard enough, Sue could conjure up the scents of roast turkey legs, hay bales, and fresh apple cider from that annual faire. She could even hear the faint sounds of minstrels performing before the royal court. The weapon had captured her eye with its intricate blood-red ouroboros on the pommel. A stark amber heptagram gleamed brightly from the black center of the ouroboros. The quillon and grip were painted black, and the scabbard was red-brown leather. She bought it, knowing exactly how she would use it and who she would use it on. By the time disaster descended upon her town from last year's mid-autumn sky, she had ground the edges and tip of the blade to a deadly sharpness. It was the final piece in her plan to skip town and leave her antagonistic, rumpot husband to rot in the swampy everglades. She just had to wait until the time was right. He was berating her for the hundredth time that morning when the ships arrived in the sky.

She had been sitting at the kitchen table, sipping on tea, ignoring the white noise of Raymond's hop-scented vitriol, so she never had the chance to see *their* actual arrival. One woman later told her that the ships just materialized out of nowhere. Others said that the spacecraft had been hidden behind thunderheads, following the hot and cold air paths and the traces of car smog into the biggest cities first. Whatever it looked like, the commotion *their* arrival caused was audible even over Ray's pathetic slurs. At first, the city rumbled with shouts of awe and pensive murmurs. Knocks on doors as neighbors pulled each other out to the streets to get a look at the first contact from an extra-terrestrial species. And then the sirens sounded. Police came to herd people into their homes as the news broke. These shiny craft of unknown origin were hovering ominously over cities around the globe. Every television program was interrupted by a government press conference giving very little detail regarding what was happening. Sue stayed inside to watch the media circus. By the end of the press conference, it had been hours since the visitors had arrived. The sun had hit its apex and was retreating to the western horizon. Ray was out back, passed out on a lawn chair mid-drink. She could leave right now, and he wouldn't even know. Hell, she could probably get rid of him now and blame it on the aliens. Her go bag was stashed beneath the creaky floorboard of their dilapidated porch. All she had to do was grab it and walk into the woods. She could leave this life forever.

But before she had a chance to break the governor's orders to stay inside, it started. She would never forget that ear-splitting noise. It began with foundation-shaking bangs, like bombs going off, louder than any gun she'd ever heard. And then, as the house rattled and shook around her, the wave of sound that ever haunted her dreams began. It resembled the teeth-grinding squeal of metal on metal, brake shoes burning away to friction, tires scraping asphalt. At first, she thought it was a car crash, but the unearthly shrieking didn't stop. A police siren, perhaps? No, it was too erratic to be that. Her stomach sank with dread as the guttural sound continued, growing louder, varying in pitch as it swept across the small city. In moments it was all too clear. The unearthly sound was coming from people. The cacophony of death swelled like an inescapable ocean siege over the county. A glance out the back window showed an unnaturally dark afternoon sky as the swarm of drop pods continued to descend from the ships. They were moving at unthinkable speeds, and Sue knew there was very little time before whatever was in those pods arrived at her home. Still, she felt frozen, and the world around her seemed to slow. Willing herself to move, Sue made a dash for the go-bag. Tennis shoes already on, she sped through the house, burst through the front door, tumbled down the stairs, and scrambled for the bag beneath the peeling decking.

She pulled and pried, but for the first time since she and Ray had moved into that godforsaken house, the damn floorboard that had tripped her countless times refused to budge. As she struggled against it, she realized the rusty, stripped nail that had been its anchor for decades was now replaced by two shiny new ones. Raymond's doing, no doubt. Had he found her go-bag? Was it still beneath the porch? She risked a glance beyond her seeding lawn as she fought a battle of wills with the ancient plank of rotting wood. All around her was chaos. The pods were still landing like meteors scarring the earth, splintering houses and flattening trees. Gunmetal hatches burst open with explosive force, and droves upon droves of biomechanical arachnids poured out from the pods. Long, spindly legs with razor-sharp points carried the extraterrestrials' massive, bulbous, hairy bodies in a parading march of inescapable doom. The smallest of them towered a good six feet above human heads, and the undersides of their thorax and opisthosoma were plated with an organic armor of some sort. Attached to their heads, above their rows of jaws and fangs, were mechanical implants where eyes should be.

As the first wave approached, the police formed a firing line and took aim at the nearest foe. Sue watched the bullets fly. Her stomach sank as its impossibly hard exoskeleton didn't even show a dent despite how much lead had been emptied into it. Some of the rounds did manage to graze the thing's front leg where it attached to the body, and the small gashes left behind started seeping ultraviolet blood. The creature let out an annoyed shriek before darting toward the uniformed men, piercing some with its sharp legs and spitting acidic web at any who had managed to jump out of the way. Massive chelicerae descended from its gaping, drooling mouth, and the monster began to feast. By now, the few people who were crazy enough to get in their cars and try to flee had abandoned them in the middle of the road, blockaded between the police cars and the massive arthropodic invaders. Some had the chance to escape their vehicles and seek cover, while others were dragged out through shattered windshields by steely mandibles. The snapping and crunching of bones punctuated the people's screams as they were eaten alive. The sound of semi-automatic weapons and shotguns peppered the air from various distances. It was every person for himself, and families watched in horror as their loved ones melted and bubbled under the unforgiving acid of poisonweb.

At last, with one final tug, the board broke beneath Sue's white-knuckled grip. She reached inside and, to her grateful surprise, found the go-bag exactly where she'd left it. The drunkard had not even noticed it when he fixed the board. And then she couldn't stop the surge of bile that rose from her stomach as she realized this was the end of life as she knew it. Stomach emptied into the hole in the porch, she started for the woods behind her house. The bag was filled with everything she needed to make it to the west coast and beyond. She jumped the side yard gate and crept to the rear edge of the house. A glance beyond the back porch indicated the invaders had not yet reached her backyard. As she silently passed through and made her way to the far fence, she paused to look back at Ray. He was still out of it, unaware of the carnage around them. Sue briefly considered taking him with her, but she knew he would only slow her down. Life with Ray was barely surviving. Survival with Ray would mean death.

"Goodbye," she whispered, sticking her right foot into a notch she'd carved in the fence and swinging her left leg over. One final look toward her past life showed a monster looming over a newly conscious Raymond. He stuttered, horrified at the sight before him. He didn't have a chance to see Sue leave him. She didn't wait around long enough to see him die. Heart pounding in her chest, she disappeared into the brush while civilization surrendered to its demise. Far behind her, Raymond's piteous cries were cut short with a juicy *squelch* as the beast bit his body in two and devoured him head-first, shredding fibrous flesh through its numerous rows of massive mandibles.

The journey west was initially supposed to take a few weeks. With full-fledged carnage and disaster sweeping across the country like a plague, weeks quickly became months. Sometimes she traveled alone; sometimes she allowed herself to have a companion or two. While some people were friendly, it was safe to assume most were not. Bands of thieves, killers, and cannibals roamed the smoldering ghost towns and vacant villages. Everywhere she went, carbon copies of her dead husband waited just around the corner to strike. But one thing was certain: when the sun set, everyone hid in silence. As the doom of their new lives took root, those who managed to survive learned more about the new species at the top of the food chain. The terminology and vernacular varied by region, but common knowledge was power against their menacing foes regardless of the words used to explain it.

When she finally reached the northern border, Sue had been lucky enough to avoid running into any more of *them*. It was rare to have traveled all that way and not come into close quarters with an "insectoid." Most people she met had not been so lucky. Thanks to kind-willed survivors, her bag had become filled with ingredients for elixirs and poultices to slow the progression of poisonweb, and she even managed to procure some makeshift armor. The beaten, repurposed metal could hopefully deflect or at least minimize any attacks from the insectoids' layered mandibles and razor-sharp legs. Like most survivors, she'd heard enough tales in dim, damp basements to know the creatures' three points of weakness. For success in combat against one of those monsters, all she needed was the element of surprise, her dagger, and a decent dose of luck. At least that's what the stories said.

Crossing the border was easy. In the before-times, Sue would have needed a passport, money, permission. But there were no such things as countries, states, or towns anymore. She crept northward through the forest, leaving minimal tracks and avoiding villages and cities. One evening she came across the outskirts of yet another municipality. Like most other places she came across, almost all buildings had been reduced to rubble. Yet somehow, despite the veritable blitzkrieg that had been the insectoids' arrival campaign, an entire shopping center on the edge of this little town remained untouched. Sue had been running low on supplies for a few days now, and she needed a new map. With the sun sinking low, she knew she would have to spend the night in the town. It was too late in the day to find a safe hiding place in the woods. Looking back on this moment, Sue would admonish herself for being sloppy. Or lazy. Or both.

She had picked a relatively large market which she figured would have the map she needed in addition to food and survival supplies. Inside, the shelves were still mostly filled with dust-covered groceries, toiletries, and food stuffs. Despite the rancid, rotting produce and meat sections, the place wouldn't make a poor spot to camp out for the night. She strolled the aisles and perused the offerings there. Grocery shopping was a luxury she no longer took for granted. Sue gathered what she needed to get by for a few more days, then scouted for a place to rest.

She decided to sleep in the manager's office that looked over the store's main floor, and as the sun disappeared behind the horizon, she drifted to sleep in a creaky, old office chair. Not an hour past dusk, she woke to a commotion downstairs.

Heart pounding in her throat, senses on high alert, Sue sprang out of sleep and into action. She unsheathed her dagger and squinted into the dark of the shop below to see who or what had found her. To her surprise, two lumbering insectoids had managed to squeeze their way into the market. Their clicking communication sent chills down her spine and she knew her luck had finally run out. Bag strapped tight against her chest, Sue quietly made her way down the narrow stairwell. She strained her ears to hear exactly where the hungry heat-seekers were in the store. The creatures were bulky, but from what she could hear, they easily managed not to knock over the rows of freestanding shelving and pyramid-stacked food cans. Sue had reached the bottom of the stairs and was contemplating a dash out the rear entrance when the purplish glow of the insectoids' bionic head-gear reflected off the tiles beneath the door to her only exit.

These insectoids had no sense of smell, but it was common knowledge that they could feel the vibration of sound with the hairs on their bodies. And thanks to the implants in their heads, they could see advanced heat signatures, just like the one Sue's nervous body was giving off. She pushed herself back up the stairs, bracing her forearms against the cool metal handrail in an attempt to bring her body temperature down to a less-detectable level. She breathed slow, step by step, returning to the office above. As quietly as she could, Sue pulled the makeshift metal helmet and breastplate from her knapsack and strapped them on. She searched the small room for anything she could use for cover.

There had been rumors of the beasts setting traps, but it was widely accepted that the newcomers were too primitive, too impulsive to create something so elaborate and forward-thinking as to trap a human being. Yet Sue had found herself in the heart of one of those preposterous snares. She waited and listened as one beast squeezed and scraped through the corridor that led past the stairwell and toward the loading docks. She breathed a sigh of relief that she would likely only have to face one of these monsters at a time. Sue shifted the desk with a loud scrape as her foe began feeling for the doorway to her stairwell with its pedipalps, the staunch hairs scraping like metal wires against the door. Kneeling between the oak desk and the one-way glass that looked over the market, Sue knew she had been found. There were only two ways this could end, and she hoped her luck had not truly run out.

The fight would not be quick. It was a battle of patience and timing as much as it was a battle of skill. Her foe had size, experience, and evolution on its side. What did she have? A dagger from the renaissance faire, common knowledge of the insectoids' weak points, and a will to live. She steadied her breathing and fought the urge to puke when she heard the grinding sound of the arthropod's hirsute, tapered legs propelling it through the stairwell. Sue sank lower into her hole between the desk and the glass and waited. A beam of purple light poured into the room as the beast peeked in through the top of the doorway, chelicerae pensively clicking as its pedipalps pushed open the door that led from the enclosed corridor into the office. Sue could see its every movement reflected in the dark glass beside her. Its large frame seeped into the room like a ghost, quiet and steady, leg by leg by leg. Low to the ground in a defensive hunting stance, the monster nearly filled the small office. Sweaty fingers tightly gripped the dagger's hilt, and she waited for the right opportunity.

The creature had likely sensed her by now. The acrid stench of poisonweb was suffocating in the close quarters of the old office. Sue prepared herself to dodge the insectoid's venomous projectile. She held her breath, battling her body's will to faint. Her vision tunneled and sweat dripped down her sides. Its reflection was stock-still, and the pensive clicking had given way to the drip-drip-drip of deadly venom trickling down its fangs and onto the ground. Why wasn't it striking? Mouth dry, Sue ventured a slow glance over the desk. She instantly regretted it.

The menacing beast had won the battle of patience. It sprang with such speed and ferocity it bounced hard against the glass behind the desk. With a wounded cry, it charged again, harder, and fought to squeeze behind the heavy oak desk, jaws snapping and stinger punching at Sue. By sheer luck, she was just out of reach of its vicious attacks. Shielded beneath the metal breastplate and her knapsack, she flattened herself against the linoleum floor and banged her pommel against the growing, spiderwebbed crack where the arthropod had made impact. Every few lunges it made, it took the slightest pause to readjust its angle. Sue worked out timing and even managed to get a few jabs in the creature's flesh where its head and abdomen met. Pushing the blade through its flesh was easier than she thought it would be. The knife smoothly slid in and out, lubricated by the arthropod's vile liquids.

But causing harm to her foe created a new complication. As lukewarm, violet blood spilled down on her, every surface became slick. She struggled to maintain her grip on her weapon. Between frantic hits against the glass and hurried stabs at the unarmored meat, Sue became aware of the desk sliding away from her. The arthropod's jaws were getting closer, and she knew time was running out. Though the crack in the glass was spreading, the window itself showed no sign of breaking anytime soon. Sue realized the creature had probably been playing with her until now, letting her believe she might have the upper hand. It could have moved the desk itself. Easier still, it could have spit poisonweb at her and avoided a fight altogether. But a live meal is so much tastier than a melted one, and what was more lively than prey that fought back?

With one final bang against the glass, Sue rolled toward the desk, ducked under the venomous bite and stinger combo it threw at her, and dashed under its legs toward the door. She ran with her dagger raised, the sharp tip slicing large gashes where the bug's legs connected to its body. More slick violet poured onto the linoleum, but her foe showed no sign of tiring. It only took a brief moment for the predator to see its prey had gotten away, and though Sue had made it down the stairs and pulled the door shut, she knew it would be mere moments before both bugs were hot on her tail. But Sue had a plan. She ran out to the main floor, where it would see her heat signature through the one-way glass. She hoped it would try to jump through the glass instead of scrambling down the stairs and battling with the difficult process of pulling open a human door.

As she made her way through the main aisle toward the front entrance, Sue heard the muted thud of her wounded enemy pouncing against the glass. Her feet hit asphalt, and the crescent moon lit her path down the road. The shattering of glass and a pained shriek echoed in the distance. Whether it had died or not, Sue knew her foe's companion would not be far behind her. It would likely be hunting her well into the morning unless she could find a stream and hide among the snowmelt currents. The plan would set her travel northward back by another week, maybe more, but if she could send herself downstream, she stood a chance of surviving long enough to make it to her destination.

Over the next weeks, Sue would live in the water, hiding from the invaders' search parties. Her pursuers combed the area on foot, searching in every crack, crevice, and hidey-hole, and when she'd managed to evade them long enough, they sent a winged complement to try and track her down from the sky. Back then, the winged scouts were a new development. Few humans believed they existed until, for nearly a week straight, the daytime air was filled with the droning sound of beating wings. The massive battalion of insectoid invaders blocked out the sun, and day was made dark as a moonless night as the invaders paraded across the sky. Many believed the display to be a declaration of victory over the planet humankind no longer had a right to call "Earth." The arthropods were considered "primitive" no more.

The sound of wings in the sky broke Sue out of her reverie. The soup was finished, the sun was high, and it was time to hunt again, but she knew she would have to settle in for the night. Her fire might have clued them in to her location, but it was unlikely based on how long it took them to fly by. Chances were high that some other nearby creature had been careless enough to pique their interest. Of course, there was also the chance they were just searching for any living food worth eating. Rabbits and ptarmigan made for small targets that easily slipped from the massive arthropod's looming grasp. If Sue remained quiet and cold enough, they probably wouldn't even think to visit her tiny little valley. Little was known about scouts, partly because they had not been part of the initial invasions. Few people had battled one of the wingless insectoids and survived, but even fewer survived an encounter with a scout. Dramatic tales of loved ones being carried off into the unknown by the winged arthropods were the new age ghost story. But as the sound of wings grew louder, something told her this was different than just a scouting mission.

The white daylight streaming in through her woven door wavered and faded to gray as the hum of countless drone wings filled the air, smoother but louder than any helicopter she'd ever heard. It was reminiscent of their victory parade all those months ago, but this time something was different. They were closer to the ground. The trees outside began to shake, and the camouflage to her burrow threatened to take flight. Once again, she strapped on her armor and bore her dagger. The scouts had never been known to hunt *per se*, but as she listened to them descending on the forest, Sue knew there was only one reason droves of drones would be touching ground this far from their nest. They were doing what so many predators do in the late autumn months. They were searching for a final feast to get them through the winter.

There was a chilling sound of hefty insect wings and thick, wire-hair sensilla scraping against foliage as the predators descended. Sue heard one land with a light splash by the small stream outside her door and braced herself for a fight to the death. Still, more were flying above, and the light was so obscured that when she peaked out between the woven branches of her doorway, she was greeted with a scene in monochrome. Amidst the low-contrast grays of the valley, pops and streams of ultraviolet purple betrayed her foes' positions as they scanned for warm sustenance. All around her, they searched, legs splayed wide, bodies crouched low to the ground, wings folded flat across their backs, searching for vibrations and heat signatures to devour. There had to be at least six just in the immediate vicinity. In her gut, Sue knew she would not survive this. Still, she refused to go down without a fight.

Her last battle had been a nightmare, riddled with rookie mistakes. She should not have survived that whole encounter. Luck really had been on her side back then. But this time, she would not lose because she was sloppy, nor because she had underestimated her foes. She would give them one hell of a fight because she had prepared to face them, giving them ample credit for the damage they could really cause her. She would lose merely because they were the better foe. As more and more of those malevolent beasts descended around her burrow from the winter sky, she knew the time had come. She steeled herself and waited until one passed by the entrance to the den with its back turned to her. Then, with all the strength she could muster, she sprinted out between the boughs and moss of her carefully-crafted entrance and lept toward its abdomen, dagger aimed for its unprotected pedicel.

The creature tried to dodge but was not fast enough. Sue thrust up into the seam of its abdomen, but the knife did not slide in and out of the meat cleanly like last time. She had to shove it in there hard and fight against the insectoid's anatomy to pull it free. Perhaps she was malnourished, or maybe the scouts just had more gristle than fat. She expected to smell the noxious acid of poisonweb and feel the searing pain of her flesh melting off the bone, but the nasty stench and the agony that inevitably followed it never came. Instead, it merely jumped to the side and hissed. It was then Sue noticed the distinct *absence* of that nasty stench. Perhaps the winged ones weren't capable of producing it. Being so close, Sue could see some vague differences between the scouts and their earthbound counterparts. Their weak points seemed to be the same, though they were thinner, with shorter legs and longer bodies. The endpoints of their legs were not sharp and pointed but covered with sandy-looking pads. Their jaws were massive, but instead of three or four sets like their wingless counterparts, this variation only had two. Each had one very large set at the fore and one smaller set closer to the head. The head itself was more prominent, appearing almost separate from the thorax. Sue wondered if there was a similar weak point to the pedicel just behind the head.

Her enemy had waited, poised to attack, threatening her with its massive jaws. They opened and closed ferociously in a threatening display of strength. Instead of the rushing attack that was often the way of the ground-types, the beast crept toward her, dancing back and forth in an attempted feint. She could feel the mechanical violet eyes of the other predators on her, watching the event unfold, likely waiting to jump in and devour her lifeless body when it ended. Sue charged, rolled, and jabbed upward again, this time behind the head. The dagger did not find its mark, skittering instead across the bony exoskeleton. She rolled to dodge the insectoid's large stinger as it stabbed at her violently from above. Somehow she managed to make it out from beneath the creature, unscathed. Heart racing, she dashed toward her burrow, scrambled up the hill, and pounced. Before the predator knew her play, she was atop its back, plunging the blade into the break in its armor just behind its head. Her foe writhed as the dagger went in and out of the soft spot. Body-wide trembling twitches, errant steps, and nonsensical wing flutters colored the insectoid's death as the sharpened tip and edges scrambled its brain and ganglia. Confused and defeated, the creature laid itself on the ground, legs curling beneath its heavy body, and accepted its death. Perhaps Sue actually stood a chance at making it to spring.

2

THE FIRST OF US

JUSTIN M. SLOAN

MEN AND WOMEN screamed as blurry images moved across the screen before the image went blank. Wu stared at the screen of the television, then flipped the channel. Again, blank. All of them were. Finally, she found one where it was static, but she could make out reporters at the desk, their language garbled. They seemed to say something about a full-on invasion, used a word that sounded like arachnids, and showed a blurred image of a tall, spindly creature with eight legs. Then the set fell and the final image was from the camera on its side, focused on darkness in the rafters, and blood spurting out to cover it before it, too, went blank.

"We get the idea," Lance Corporal Laghari said, shutting off the television. She had just joined Corporal Constance Wu on shift for their midnight operations watch duty. They were likely safe within the Specially Compartmentalized Information Facility (SCIF), but the thought wasn't enough to put Wu's nerves at ease. Especially when considering the rest of their friends and family out there.

For a long moment, Laghari stood there with her hands

on her hips, staring at the blank screen. Finally, she turned back to Wu and shook her head. "Dammit, I wish you'd left me that last piece now."

"What? Pizza?"

"I'm just saying, if I'm going to die..."

"You'd want your last meal to be a slice of cold pizza. This is so... so fucked! People are dying out there!"

No response.

"Sorry," Wu finally said. "If it makes you feel any better, this SCIF is damn secure. The door's eight inches thick of metal, the walls set to withstand heavy attacks. If anyone has a chance, it's us."

Movement caught their attention from the security displays. A blur, and then one of the displays went dark. Wu's heart raced, her thoughts quickly going to dark places, and then she reached out for comfort, not even realizing what she was doing until Leghari's hand was held firmly in her own. A shot sounded from outside, and just when Wu was about to let go of the hand, she gripped it tight with both of her own. Leghari didn't appear to mind, other than the bit of discomfort she seemed to be having, judging by her scrunched-up face. Then again, maybe that was fear?

"Is this some end of the world, apocalypse shit?" Leghari asked.

All Wu could do was shake her head, trying to get her mouth to move but finding it too dry for words to come out. Apparently sensing this, Leghari gave her hand a squeeze, pulled away, and came back a second later with Wu's half-drunk bottle of Pepsi.

Wu took a drink, then managed, "Thanks."

"No problem." Leghari shook out her hand, then eyed Wu with concern. "We're going to get through this."

A laugh escaped Wu's lips, though she wore no smile. "This? You don't even know what this is?"

"But... together..."

Wu gulped, and nodded, seeing fear in the other woman's eyes. Leghari clearly needed her as much as Wu needed Leghari. Another shot, then several went off, and something flew into view on one of the cameras. A round object.

"Is that...?" Leghari started, then turned and retched. Wu wasn't far behind, though the retching didn't come—she wanted any excuse to not look at the screen where she was fairly certain that object had been a head. She held the other woman's hair back as spittle fell into the garbage can to join the yellow vomit there from the first expulsion.

"Come on, we've... seen worse," Wu tried.

At least that got a scoff out of Leghari. "Worse? When?"

"I mean..." Wu didn't want to mention the destruction they'd seen when an IED had gone off beneath their HUMVEE when stationed in the Congo. There was a reason some Marines rode on their helmets, and they'd seen that reason first-hand that day. Unlike then, though, they'd at least known their enemy then. Here, neither had a clue what was happening other than the brief blurs they had seen on the news and security cams, and from what they'd seen then, it appeared to be some sort of monster or alien attack.

BAM! A thud from the front doors pulled her out of the thoughts, and Wu stood abruptly, eyeing the fire axe in its spot on the wall. There were two rifles and two pistols in the SCIF, but locked away and she didn't have access.

Suddenly, the door opened!

"Shit," she muttered, then took a step back, breath halting.

"You in here?" a voice said, and then the door was open and a face appeared. A high-and-tight haircut, hard eyes that shone green in the fluorescent light, and a meaty hand pulling the door open. It was Staff Sergeant Jones, and she was ecstatic to see him. He eyed them both, nodded, and shouted, "Wu, cover us!"

"Cover...?" A horrific shrieking came from behind him, and he threw the door open as he tossed her the rifle. She lunged forward, caught it, then went to the door to see that he was dragging another Marine, Sergeant Wyatt, behind him. A line of blood went to the stairs, and there, rising up from the darkness of those stairs, was one of the creatures. Only now it wasn't a blur. Instead, it was rocky carapace, reminding her of a massive cross between a crab and a spider, dark and with strange blue and orange growths on its back. She wanted to scream, to throw herself to the ground and curl up in a ball to forget this horrible dream. Instead, her training kicked in and she braced herself, rifle at the ready, and sent off a three-round burst from the M-16. Then another, and another, until Jones was there shouting for her to cease-fire while he got the door closed.

It slammed shut, and all knew it wouldn't open without someone knowing the code. Hell, that door was built to withstand heavy assaults. That didn't stop Wu from yelping when the creature on the other side started its attack. Leghari was there, though, pulling her back into the ops watch section of the SCIF, where Jones was lifting Wyatt up into a chair.

"Someone get pressure on this Marine," Jones said, and once Wu did so, he took off for the back of the room to retrieve the first-aid kit.

For the first time, Wu noticed the rifles slung over Wyatt's shoulder. She helped lower them off while Jones applied gauze to a nasty wound on the other man's side. Wyatt had his pack, Jones, too.

"You came prepared," Wu noted.

"We saw the news and I'm always prepared," Jones said, finishing off the gauze. Nodding at the rifles, he added, "Figured we might need this. Area for concern—the armory was unmanned."

"Something tells me that's not high on the list of concerns."

"What the hell's going on out there?" Laghari demanded.

"Hell if we know," Jones said. "Those things are attacking, and we... we're going to do our damned best to survive." He moved to check the message they'd called him about, and his face went pale. Finally, he swiveled to the phone and picked it up to dial, but after a second, put it back down. "Try your cellphones. Line's dead."

They all did—and all went to busy signals. The banging outside the door returned, and Wu found Leghari's hand in hers again. It continued like that for hours, even as Wu and the others took stock and arranged the wall of MREs in one corner of the storage closet, where they had a wall of water that had been delivered recently.

All three shared looks of concern, all likely wondering the same thing—how long this could last.

The answer to how long they were able to hold out on those MREs, along with first their water supplies and then that from the pipes—luckily—was three damned years. And they were damned. First had come the infection, and Wyatt had nearly recovered before one day not waking up again. He had still been with them for another couple of days, and Jones had talked about making a run for help, but they all knew that would be a death sentence for him.

At least the damn creature outside had stopped trying to get in through the front door after a few weeks. There had been other times when Wu heard scraping noises, but nothing had ever broken in. Power remained on, though the air seemed stale. Plumbing worked, and the SCIF had showers in the bathrooms, for Marines to use after a good run. Recently the water had turned slightly brown, though, and they had all taken to showering less. Since they couldn't exactly go for a run or do much that much in terms of exercise, it wasn't much of a concern. At most they would do pushups and use the pullup bar, and Jones did some version of CrossFit when he felt up to it, but lately, even he had been slow to motivate himself to work out.

Now that they were on the last two MREs, they came to the realization that their time simply surviving had come to an end. Wu almost felt relieved. Death didn't sound so bad compared to this monotonous routine, and she felt her insides rebelling after so long surviving this way.

"Straws?" Laghari offered when Jones said they would need to do an MRE run.

"No, I'm going," he countered.

"Because you're a man?" Laghari flipped him off. "Not how it works here, big guy."

Jones glared. "I'm going."

"Straws it is," Wu chimed in, agreeing. They had them ready, knowing something like this would come up. Laghari grabbed them up, held out her hand, and forced Jones to take one. He did, and held it up—one of the long ones. Next came Wu, and she took the short one.

She stared at the straw in her hand, realizing she'd

known it would be her. Wanted it to be, even. This was her chance to see what was out there, to breathe fresh air. And possibly, to die.

"You know, it's funny," Wu said. "All those years bitching about the commissary, living in the barracks, getting experimental shots... None of it mattered in the end, and I'd take it all over this hell we've lived through."

"Damn straight," Laghari agreed.

"This is horse shit," Jones cut in. "Wu, stay put, I'm pulling rank and—"

"Rank doesn't exist anymore," Laghari cut him off. "Wu pulled short, so... it's her call."

Wu had never been the type to back down, and didn't now. "Maybe it's all over out there, and everyone simply forgot to tell us?"

Jones glared, not humored by that thought one bit, apparently.

Laghari put a hand on Wu's shoulder. "We can all go."

"And then we all die. Not a chance." Wu already had the packs ready—one on the front, one for the rear, so that she could stockpile. "You two, stay safe."

"Back at you," Jones replied, looking helpless at the idea of staying put while she did this.

"Constance..." Leghari said, using Wu's first name for the first time, but she didn't have anything else to add. She simply stood there, arms folded around her torso, and bit the side of her lower lip.

"I'll be fine," Wu said, and approached the front door. The other two stood ready with rifles. Considering that they had tried this once before only to be met by three of those arachnid creatures and barely managed to get the door closed—after exposing Wyatt's body—this was a smart precaution.

The door opened and a horrible stench caught in Wu's nostrils. She steeled her nerves, then cautiously stepped out toward the stairs. No sign of the arachnids yet. What she did find, though, was what looked like a half of a rib cage. When she realized that it was all that remained of Wyatt, she almost wanted to run back into the SCIF and hide. She needed to do this, though. For the other two, and to prove that she was still a Marine at heart.

Going to the stairs, she dry heaved at the sight of dried blood and some sort of strange overgrowth that reminded her of the material used to fill gaps in a house. Caulks, was it? She figured some of the smell was coming from that, and as she walked past it, realized she was looking at some sort of fungus. At the bottom of the stairs it was a sprawling ocean of orange, white tendrils reaching out from it in all directions and growing up the walls and over cars. Parts of the land were clear, as if spread by Moses and it was the red sea—only, in this case, orange.

She started working her way through the areas of ground that weren't touched, noting that all vegetation in this area was completely dead. That smell was horrific, exacerbated by the heat. Sweat trickled down her back as she crouched, moving slowly in case the arachnids were close.

A car in her path gave her reason to pause. Two corpses were inside, the orange fungus having moved through a crack in the window and taken them. It grew both on them and from within, causing bits of their flesh to hang loose and expose the internal fungus, blood long ago dried. Her eyes welled up, but she refused to let any tears fall. Not yet, at least. Not until her mission was over. Quickly finding a way around the car, she started moving faster toward the barracks and supply depot. She had to hope to God nobody else had raided the MREs yet. At this point, she was so exposed that she had no doubt the arachnids would take her out if there were any around. From what she could see, they weren't. And rightly so, as this fungus had seemingly taken out any chance for food they might have had.

Wu reached the supply depot, ducking in and finding more fungus, more half-exposed and rotting, torn apart corpses. To linger and look at them would have been her end, she knew. A lifetime of nightmares would already no doubt follow.

She went straight for the closet where she had last obtained MREs before a mission, kicked fungus from a door, and stared. Nothing! She had failed. Taking a deep breath, she found her calm, then assessed her surroundings. A truck had fungus on it, but was closed. She moved over to it, found the lever, and managed to kick it unstuck. When she got the door open, she gasped. The fungus hadn't managed to get in, and there were several packs within. She pulled herself up, checked the first, and found several MREs. The next as well. Quickly transferring them to her own, she then gave herself a pat on the back, since there wasn't anyone else there to do so.

She stood at the edge of the truck, looking out at the fungus and its strange tendrils, and shook her head. There was nothing else for her here, and quite honestly, nothing else in the vicinity. She didn't hear a single arachnid or any other living soul. Without a doubt, nobody was coming for them, and that meant that if she and the others were going to survive, it wouldn't be stuck in a SCIF. She would have to convince them it was time to leave.

Making her way back was quicker because she had less fear slowing her down, and soon she was in the watch room, showing off her findings.

"Well done, Corporal," Jones said, clearly refusing to drop the whole rank thing.

"Thanks." She took a deep breath, about to put forth her argument to leave, when a dizzy spell came over her. The room shifted, seemed to spin, then went dark.

She had no idea how long she'd been out, but when she opened her eyes again, she was on her sleeping bag up where she'd been sleeping in one of the cubicles on the main floor. It had been decorated with cutouts from a magazine she'd found in one of the desks, and had notes written but never sent to her parents. She had no idea what had happened to them. Since power and cell service had cut off so soon and with them being halfway across the country, she had no hope of finding out anytime soon.

"Laghari?" she said, pushing herself up with a groan. When no response came, she reached out to the desk for stability, but then froze there, staring at her hand. Small bits of orange growth showed around the base of her fingernails, and white lines appeared as if veins under her skin. Her next breath was forced, and she had to remind herself to breathe. Again, she called out, "Leena?"

"Help," came a muffled sound, and Wu wondered if she'd heard it a few seconds ago. Again it sounded, louder now, and she charged back into the operations room, where what she found horrified her. That orange growth covered one wall, bubbling out in sections, hard in others, and with those white tendrils connected to Jones. He sat in the middle of the room, one leg up, covered in shit and piss, and that orange fungus grew from his mouth and out of one side of his head. His skull appeared to be cracked by it, but his eyes moved over to see her!

His mouth, not yet hindered, managed, "Kill me."

She took a step back, horrified, only to run into

something. With a scream she turned, thrashing as hands took her. For a moment all went black, then came into focus, and she realized she was clinging to pipe along the top of the nearby wall, Laghari on the floor, crawling away and looking back in horror. The woman's eyes were wide, tints of orange there.

"No..." Wu muttered, dropping to the floor and collapsing to her knees. She looked at her hands, back to Laghari, and shuddered. "Did I... attack you?"

"What the hell?" Laghari stammered, then pushed herself to her feet. "Are you... you?"

"I—I think so."

"You went all wild, thrashing about, striking me. It's taking over."

"It?" Wu glanced over to the fungus on the wall, leading out from the operations room and along a wall that led down to the rest of the building. She didn't need an answer —she could see it right there.

A grunt sounded from the other room, and Wu didn't even need to think about her next move. She stormed over to the locker where they kept the weapons, and pulled out a pistol. A quick check showed it was loaded, so she stepped into the operations room and raised it.

"Wu..." Laghari didn't say anything more. She wasn't going to protest, and even if she had insisted on being the one to pull the trigger, Wu wouldn't have let her.

"I'm sorry," Wu muttered, switching off the safety, aiming, and then squeezing the trigger. As shitty as she had been at the rifle, she had always been an expert marksman with the pistol. Three shots left Jones in a pile of orange and red, and she turned then, lifting the pistol to her own head.

At this, Laghari cut in, pushing the pistol aside. "No."

"We'll end up like him. I won't allow it."

"You don't know that."

Wu's arm went limp, her moment of bravery over, and she let Laghari take the pistol. Her resolve wasn't yet completely gone, though, so Wu said, "If it starts—you promise we'll do it. Together."

Laghari nodded. "Except, I saw you. You had it before he did, and it... didn't do to you what it did to him. For some reason, it hasn't done the same to either of us."

Wu gulped, then nodded. Her eyes went to that pipe along the upper wall, and she frowned. "How did I...?"

"I wondered that as well. Plus, the hit you landed? That was a force I've never felt." She rubbed her side, then lifted up her cammies to reveal a nasty bruise—purple, with an outline of orange. As they stared, though, the purple faded.

"We're infected, if that's what you can call it," Wu said. "But it's having a very different effect on us. For now, anyway."

"For now," Laghari agreed, lifting up the pistol to look at it. She set it down on the counter, then, and took Wu's hands. "I don't know what it is... maybe some of the shots the Marines gave us, ones they used on younger Marines, but not Jones? Or maybe it has to do with that plus us being females? No clue, but I know one thing—I'm not sticking around here and waiting it out. Are you with me?"

"Where would we go?" Wu asked.

"Anywhere. Search for a place that's not... like this." She nodded to the orange fungus. "See if we can find others. My mom, your parents. Anyone."

Wu felt her friend's hand in hers, the warmth flowing between them. It was unlike anything she had ever felt before, and in that moment, craved more contact with her. She leaned in, gently touching her lips to Laghari, and found the other woman both receptive and encouraging.

Their lips parted, tongues meeting, and then a moment of passionate kissing before Wu pulled back, and nodded.

"As long as you promise we stick together, I'm in."

Laghari agreed, and they quickly went about preparing for the trip, with rifles, pistols, and filling their packs with whatever they could find. They were going to brave the world out there, but before they exited, Wu took Laghari in for one last kiss, smiled, and said, "For luck."

3

OCHER SPRING

JB LETTERCAST

The Courier

AFTER DAYS of endless rain and soaked-through clothing, there was finally a break in the clouds. The caravan traveling with Doctor Marius LaPorte had managed to make it to the lowland, which sprawled out before them like a lush, green carpet against the dark, steely sky. The travelers soaked in the brief moments of sun between passing clouds. It was possibly their last chance at true, dry warmth. Pauses between downpours had grown shorter and less frequent, and the ground would only become soggier as they neared their destination.

Normally, Marius would not leave his home in Hillfar. It was elevated, safe, and usually dry, even in the wet season. But his friend and colleague, Doctor Angela Reyes, had sent a courier from the swamp-town of Furnmoss with intriguing news that promised to make this hellacious trek well worth the discomfort.

In her letter, Angela suggested the possibility of developing a biological weapon against the Arachnids. The dastardly beings had landed on Earth years ago and caused death and carnage beyond imagining, and they still ruled over the land. Marius had barely survived the arrival of the alien species. Before *they* had come, he'd spent most of his time at the laboratory, studying cases of virus strain mutations, content to go home and relax when his work was done.

Ever since the world ended, he had taken to hiding himself in the medicinal side of his craft, treating wounds and formulating ointments for those who made it to Hillfar Fastness from the wasteland that was once civilization. It was still not uncommon to hear news of a settlement vanishing off the map, and he was constantly reminded of the virulent harm those Arachnid bastards could do. Memories of loved ones and colleagues meeting their brutal, violent demise haunted him every moment of every day, even as he brought others back from the brink of death.

He knew leaving his post, even for a few weeks, was a massive risk. But as afraid as he was of leaving the safety of his nest of paperwork and salves, he was twice as angry at those monstrosities for choosing Earth as their new home. If there was a chance to conjure something that would help his fellow man defend against their attacks, he wanted to be the one to make it. And so, he went.

The caravan was still a few days from the Oar's Chapel region, where Furnmoss and other backwater towns like it made burrows in the boggy forest. He'd heard tales of the colorful characters in that far-west region, so brazen they made their homes mere kilometers from an Arachnid nest, strategically sheltering themselves from attacks by nesting deep within the bayhead. He was uncertain how Angela, known for her practicality and sensible demeanor, had ended up in a place like that.

Marius took in the passing landscape from the rear of the wagon. The rattle of wheels on deteriorating concrete, paired with the snore of his apprentice, Yosef, and the *clop clop clop* of hooves as oxen pulled them along, all conjured ponderings of old settlers heading west toward a better life. He scribbled a few notes in his journal, questions he wanted to explore when he arrived at Furnmoss, and hopped off the wagon to stretch his legs and warm his back in the sun.

The scent of precipitation was on the wind, and he could see the next barrage of rain barreling toward them, swiftly closing the distance across the plain. Even as the sun began to vanish behind the growing mass of clouds, his clothes were dryer than they'd been since the day they headed west. It was a relief.

From the front of the caravan, a few wagons ahead, Marius heard someone call a halt.

It was likely the mountaineer who led these caravans hither and thither from coast to coast, a real wild-west gal by the name of Hemsworth. As Marius began to make his way up the wagon train, urgent cries of *"Doctor!"* and *"Medic!"* came downwind. And, though he could not be entirely sure, he thought he heard the word *"Chaplain!"* among them. Before he could get close enough to assess the scene, Hemsworth approached.

"Doc," she said, a handkerchief held to her face, "something real vile up ahead. I'll get the looky-loos cleared back so you can have room to work."

"What happened up there, Hem? Did one of the kids get run over? Or is it bugs we're dealing with?" He reached for his medical pouch, always strapped tightly to his chest.

"I... well, some poor fella seems to be hurt somehow. I'm not too sure we can help him. Bein' honest, I saw something so gruesome in all my travels on this road." She turned and cleared out the few of the crowd who had managed to hold their stomachs long enough to get a good look at the grizzly sight.

Marius lifted his own handkerchief to his face in preparation for whatever had bystanders retching into a ditch by the wagons, then stepped toward the tall orange stalk planted in the middle of the road. It stood about five feet tall, then stooped heavy with a swollen, fuzzy bulb at its tip. It resembled many fungi he had studied in his laboratory, with one exception: it stood nearly as tall as a covered wagon. As he neared it, his eyes wandered the body of the protuberance, following it down to where it had taken root. Horror filled his chest, followed quickly by the dizzying, intoxicating rush of scientific intrigue. He paused when the nauseating scent of decay hit him, regained his composure, then got even closer.

Beneath the rather tall fungus was the sprawling, tortured, quite rancid body of a human being, surprisingly void of insect life despite having rotted there for a few days at the very least. Marius deduced that the ocher fungus had planted itself in the person's face via spore -- perhaps in a nostril or mouth -- and sprouted out through an orifice. The weight of the stalk alone had likely collapsed the viscerocranium. Sprawling root-like tendrils, ranging from deep red to a brown-ocher to a putrid off-white, traveled out from the base of the fungus and enveloped the person down to their midsection, plastering them seamlessly to the road.

"I don't think they're alive," he called back to the crowd. Even as he said this, he saw a hand twitch, fingers grabbing unnaturally at the concrete, shearing a fingernail or two off already raw fingertips. If this person was alive, it was barely. He knelt, twisting to look the corpse square in the eyes. "You poor creature," he sighed.

The scraping sound of fingers again. A muffled groan, impossibly quiet beneath the five feet of fungus spiraling up like a tower from the person's face. A mizzling rain began to patter on the busted pavement. Marius pulled out a tape measure from his pouch and eyed the thick base of the stalk.

And then it happened.

The fungus moved.

It started as a small ripple through the tendrils. They curled up and shook like the tentacles of a furious squid, then gripped the ground once more. In an astonishing fraction of an instant, the ripple traveled up the roots, up the stalk, a quake that echoed toward the bulb. With a shudder, the fungus became erect, looming over him at nearly twice his height. No longer drooping, the bulb at the tip of the fungus quivered, somehow becoming larger and more full. From his low perch, Marius understood and made a mad break for it.

"Run!" he shouted, scrambling back toward the caravan.

He was too late.

South

"Are you sure you have to leave, Ange?" The Draycott mayor's pining was beginning to grate on Angela's nerves. All the more reason to go.

"Yes, Lawrence. I have done all I can for your settlement, and it really is time for me to move on. Also, please call me Doctor." It was the thousandth time that week she'd reminded him of her status. The world may have ended, but titles still held meaning.

Despite her protests, Lawrence heckled her all the way out from her makeshift lab in Draycott's old butchery, through the town courtyard, down to the town entrance, never once calling her "Doctor." The sealed gate required approval to open for anyone to enter or depart. She stopped and looked up at the attendant, Sal, of whom she'd grown quite fond. They exchanged a bittersweet glance as Lawrence continued to drone on in the background, ignored.

"Very well then. Seeing as you're already packed and halfway out the door, I guess there's no use in stopping you." He let the phrase hang in the air, clearly hoping Angela would change her mind. But not even gorgeous Salanna Johannesson could make her want to plant roots in this dull town. With a sigh of defeat, Lawrence waved to the gate attendant. "Open the gates, Sal!" With a tearful grin, Sal pulled the clinking crank for the rolling steel gate. For the first time in ages, Doctor Angela Reyes stepped out of the stale air of the housing dome into pure, unfiltered sunlight.

As the gate closed behind her, she could hear Sal's soft voice. "Be safe on your travels."

"I'll never forget you and your... very pale... town," Angela said, half to no one, half to Sal, who probably could not even hear her behind the metal shell encasing the settlement.

Angela was not good at goodbyes, but she was terribly good at leaving.

Just a few weeks ago, she received a request to travel south to the bayhead area of Oar's Chapel. A town by the name of Furnmoss had made her an offer she could not refuse. They had access to a university's science lab and offered her a residency there. The only problem? Furnmoss' proximity to an Arachnid nest -- several nests, actually.

Normally this would deter her from making any effort to get close. Settlements in Furnmoss's position rarely lasted a few months before being invaded by hungry mega-bugs. Except Furnmoss had stayed standing -- had been growing even -- for just over a year. According to Furnomss' mayor, the Arachnids rarely attacked the town. In fact, the only ones that came near it seemed sickly and decrepit. And *that* was the catch. There was always a catch.

Angela lived her life by her title. Her name brought her all over the map. She bounced between settlements, using her knowledge of infrastructure and technology to get towns to the next stage of development. Her price? Access to something new and interesting. She wanted to gain novel knowledge she could use to improve humanity's fight against the alien invaders humanity had come to call *the Arachnids*.

Some towns offered training in medical procedures like venom extraction and the acidweb healing process. Others offered pieces of scrap from Arachnid augmentations for studying and attempts at reverse engineering. Everywhere she went, she added a new trunk for the booklets she filled with all sorts of useful knowledge. Furnmoss offered her a home base at the university campus, plus a chance to rub shoulders with sickly Arachnids. The potential in their promise was off the scales, and she hoped they could deliver.

No one in their right mind would willingly travel to Oar's Chapel, but here she was, making the trek with her three apprentices and a small train of wagons and livestock to transport her effects. The boondock town was a good two weeks away from her current perch in the flat lands, and she knew the ride would be more than rough. But this tour was once in a lifetime. Furnmoss offered her a chance to study two important pieces of the Arachnid puzzle. First, an anomaly. The bugs didn't attack the town. The nest near

Furnmoss was obviously dealing with some sort of ailment in their population. Second, the dead and dying bugs often wandered near the town and the road. This offered a chance to recover a complete piece of Arachnid tech, which had never been successfully accomplished.

Lastly, Furnmoss offered her what Draycott and so many of the flatland colonies did not: fresh air. Sure, it would be dank, swampy air, but it was bound to be better than the stale, recycled air she'd been breathing for the past three months. At that thought, she reveled in the spotty sunlight that poked between thick, heavy clouds as the caravan started forward. The air buzzed with the electricity of thunderstorms in the north. With the wind in their sails, the wagon train made its way south toward Oar's Chapel.

Oar's Chapel

Late in their journey to the bayhead, in the final hours of a gray afternoon, Angela tried to focus on a piece of literature amidst the tussle and jostle of her wagon. One of the wheels had broken just three days in, and while the patch job had been decent, she knew it was only a matter of time -- mere hours, perhaps -- before it gave out for good. An even darker gray cloud rolled toward the sun, gradually taking most of her reading light. She lit a lantern, but with all its swaying back and forth, she only managed to catch every fourth word. Angela liked to travel, but on day sixteen of a thirteen-day trip, an exciting journey easily became tiresome.

With a sigh, she tucked her papers back into the water-resistant trunk at the center of the wagon. There was precipitation on the air -- and on every other surface imaginable. Her clothes and papers stank of mildew, and her boots squished with dampness. She was in dire need of a hot fire and four solid walls. Just a little while longer, and they would finally be at Furnmoss.

An escort party had been waiting for them at the entrance to the Oar's Chapel region, adding three extra wagons to their train. They were unlike any wagons she had seen in the plains or even along the coast. These were tactical units, complete with their own armed militia. Each wagon carried four militia members -- two to drive it and two to operate the slingshot mounted atop it. One would mount and light the slingshot's ammunition, and the other would aim and fire it.

Angela understood that this type of militia escort was common courtesy in Oar's Chapel. The Furnmoss governor, Tomás, had given her the rundown on all Oar's Chapel's safety procedures in his very lengthy request for her residency at their university. But despite the warriors accompanying them to what they called "the mouth of Oar's Chapel," Angela and her company found it hard to be at ease. The knowledge that they were passing through a densely populated neighborhood of Arachnids was very difficult to get used to.

The caravan would be stopping soon to turn in for the night, so Angela hopped out of her wagon to stretch her legs and walk beside the driver she'd grown rather fond of. Elias had been her travel companion for some years now. Content to follow the doctor wherever she roamed, he traveled light and reveled in the opportunity to see the world. It didn't hurt that he knew just about everything there was to know about how to get from here to there. When he came into her life, he was by no means a practiced mountaineer. But something about the thirty-something drifter had struck her as worth keeping around. Each night and morning, they engaged in a friendly -- occasionally feisty -- round of small talk, tapering off into comfortable, familiar silence as the day or night wore on.

The miserable drizzle that had begun around midday had not yet ceased. Angela felt the droplets become fatter, heavier, and somehow more menacing in the time it took for her to reach Elias' perch at the head of the wagon.

"It's getting quite gross out today," she began.

"That's all you have to say to me?" he replied in mock offense.

"What do you mean?"

"No cool science fact about microbes in mud? No geothermal engineering joke to cheer me up after a hard day's work?"

"I hate to disappoint, but if I'd known your reckless driving would add an extra four days to our travel, I would have stocked up on more facts. We're plum out of that kind of rations here!" The two shared a warm chuckle, and the sun, hidden by a great wall of quite gloomy storm clouds and a treeline that stretched on for ages, kissed the horizon. Feeling the fingers of anxiety tickle her collarbone, Angela eyed the trees framing the muddy road. "It's almost dark. When do you think we should call it quits, El?"

"Soon. Just need to find a spot off the road to hitch the wagons. I bet our escorts have a checkpoint somewhere nearby."

"I'll pop over and give them an ask then. You just hang out here and look pretty," she said with a playful wink, turning on her heel to make her way through the muck to one of the escort wagons. Just as she reached the closest wagon, which was ahead of the wagon she shared with Elias, the driver called a halt.

There was a swaying rustle in the mangrove in the

distance, and Angela's blood ran cold. Swiftly, she dashed to the far side of the wagon, kneeling low behind a wheel. From there, she could just make out the ghastly shape making its way through the mizzle and fog. A hush fell over the travelers; the calm before the storm. Drivers dismounted to steady their pack animals. The escorts made ready for a fight.

The flaming shots were prepared in a factory long before the soldiers loaded them up as ammunition on the road. From what she understood, they were simple ceramic balls filled with oil, swaddled in incendiary-soaked rags. She reckoned the biggest task was probably moving the cumbersome ammo from their storage to the catapult, though she assumed aiming such a finicky weapon at the typically quick Arachnid targets was not easy either. Normally, time was of the essence when dealing with the mega-bugs, but Angela almost felt sorry for the ambling shell of a thing struggling to make its way to the road.

The weapon was locked and loaded well before the creature was close enough to hit without risking wasting the shot on a tree trunk. The purple glow of its biomechanical augmentation pierced the fog as it moved, and behind it was the shimmer of a second set of augmented optics. It was well known that they hunted in pairs and packs of three, and for a moment it looked like the caravan had met their demise.

Except, hunting parties usually moved swiftly, efficiently. This second Arachnid seemed to be moving just as slow as the first. Was it dying, too? Angela imagined a parade of diseased mega-bugs making the pilgrimage away from their nest to die in peace. The first one slowed as it reached the road, then collapsed into the ditch that separated the trail from the wilderness. Pitifully, its tarsus scraped against the broken concrete of the old road. It groaned helplessly, lying in a dilapidated heap mere meters from the caravan.

Angela, still crouched behind the wagon, turned to the soldier beside her. He was coated in the eye-watering stench of incendiary. With a choking cough, she whispered, "Why didn't you guys shoot it yet?"

"That one won't hurt us; it's too weak," he responded.

"Then what's the catapult for?"

"Insurance."

"Insurance?"

"Just watch," he said, gesturing for her to stand up. She glanced down the caravan at El, who stood just behind one of his oxen. The sun had almost completely descended, and between the lanterns, the torches, and the warm bodies, Angela feared their fate was as good as sealed. They were as visible as they could possibly get to the heat-seeking predators. Dying or not, they probably still had an appetite, and the second Arachnid had yet to slow down. She was about to be some space bug's dinner.

"I think we really should go," she said, venturing above a whisper. "Go on, fire that thing so we can make a break for it!" Her voice cracked with desperation. The animals began to stir, and drivers fought to keep them calm. The second Arachnid was almost to the road now, and her heart threatened to pound right up her throat and out of her mouth.

"Not yet. Tomás told us to show you what happens to the dying ones when they reach the end of their usefulness to the hive."

These people were really messed up in the head if this was what they did for entertainment! Angela could only imagine what she was about to see. The healthy Arachnid towered over the body of the sickly one and began to chatter with it. The clicking and chirping went on for about a minute. It was common knowledge that the bugs could communicate in various ways, this being the least common. The language was used sparingly enough that she'd never known of any successful attempts at translating it. Still, there was something intimate about whatever these monsters were saying to each other.

Angela scolded herself for humanizing the things. Soon enough, the chattering stopped. After a moment of silence, the tinkering began. It was too dark to know exactly how it transpired, but in a few moments, the biomechanical headgear that had augmented the dying -- *dead?* -- Arachnid's vision was disabled and removed from its head. From the sound of it, it was not a painless procedure. The wails the mega-bug let out at the onset of the ghastly procedure were purely haunting, and Angela knew she would never forget them.

At the end of it, the creature lay listless in the ditch on the side of the road. Its companion turned its back on the smorgasbord of live flesh laid out for it *right there on the road*, and headed back toward the nest, technology safely retrieved from its diseased comrade. In moments it vanished into the dark of the marshland, and the only sound Angela could hear was the crackle of the fire in the lanterns and the pitter-patter of evening rain. The fire shot was placed atop the bug carcass and set alight, and the tired caravan continued onward through the dark sludge of the boggy night for several more hours until they reached a place to make camp.

Next stop, Furnmoss.

Furnmoss

As midday broke on their final day of travel, half a day after she witnessed what she had dubbed *The Oar's Chapel Phenomenon*, she took in the sights of the burgeoning settlement that really should not have existed in such an unforgiving place. It had an air of magick around it -- and it wasn't all pleasant magick, either.

As the party passed through the gates, it became obvious that their wagons would have to remain parked near the entrance of the town. Just a half kilometer in, the beaten path vanished into the marshy muck. Angela was surprised to see that much of the town was on stilts, muddy water lapping at the bases of the businesses and homes. In place of roads, boardwalks had been laid out, and toward the heart of the place, the mossy boards became broad causeways and piers along wandering canal streets.

The town itself was much bigger than she anticipated, and it was surprisingly unguarded. Though some weak-looking fences outlined the Furnmoss territory, it seemed the entire settlement was left exposed to the westerly mangroves and marsh. It was unlike any settlement she'd visited, a profound change from the densely sheltered dome of Draycott. The townspeople paid their exposed flank little mind. Some even took boats out into the water to catch fish and eels.

On Angela's journey to Furnmoss, herds and herds of black and gray clouds traveled with them to their destination. It seemed all those big stormy bodies had made their home in the swamp town itself. Some loomed high above, dousing the sun. Others sank way down low, mingling like ghosts among the dingy market stalls. The air was thick with dampness, hoods of moss densely coated the roofs of the cobblestone houses, and the scent of something perplexing meandered in the breeze.

At a glance, the place looked surprisingly quiet for as many buildings as were there. For a moment, as the escort detail departed and the gates closed behind them, Angela wondered if she had made a mistake coming to such a spooky place. All around the outskirts of the town were dense pockets of trees. It was not unreasonable to think that at any moment, a scout team of Arachnids could come waltzing in and chomp a person in half. Anxiously, she followed Elias and the others toward the ox pen and stable, just to the east of the town gates. She was just about to smash a mosquito the size of a 50-cent piece when she heard the *slosh-poc! slosh-poc!* of rushing footsteps behind her.

"You must be Doctor Reyes!"

She turned, forcing a grin. "And you must be--"

"Tomás! The governor," he twanged. "Welcome to my humble home!" He extended his hand, and she shook it firmly.

"Quite the place you have here, Tomás."

"She's a beaut, eh? A real gem!"

"Was it *your* idea to build a town this close to a nest?"

Tomás gawked and gave a wry laugh. "Furnmoss has been here since before the bugs came! We just converted her. Speaking of the times before, let's get you settled into your new office. University is this way." He gestured, stomping off toward the town.

Angela had to speedwalk to keep up with the large man's strides. Tomás towered over her and the short townspeople. He pointed out different landmarks and made brief introductions as they went, not taking any meaningful time to stop and make her acquaintance. It seemed he pointed out a new landmark, a new store, a new denizen with each breath as they wound their way through the strange labyrinth that was the town center. Eventually, Angela had to stop and catch her breath.

"It's no worry, Doc. I'm glad we stopped here," he said, leaning with the swagger of a proud papa on the damp wall of a tavern. "Furnmoss has never been big on tourism, but we were a research town in before-times. This here was my pride and joy!"

Angela glanced up at the sign swaying in the light breeze. "*The Tinker Inn, Tavern.*"

"Yes, ma'am! This is where you and your folk have rooms, if you choose to accept them. Some visitors prefer to sleep in their wagons, close to the gates, but if you ask me, this is the safest place in town. We serve breakfast in the morning and liquor at night!"

"Wow, thank you. Such hospitality!" Her first impressions of the town had been those of gloom and glower, but perhaps the people here would make up for all that through generosity of spirit.

"I can't wait to show you the university! It was mainly a water research facility back in the day, so it's out on the water, still a short way from here. Would you like to see your room here first, or...?"

Angela had finally caught her breath and wanted to revel in the bit of afternoon sun that had managed to break through the clouds. Her lungs burned just slightly with exertion, but the damp air soothed them. After more than two weeks of sitting on a wagon, the brisk walk was that pleasant kind of almost-too-much. "Oh, no, I can see my room when the rest of my crew see theirs. Lead the way, Tomás!"

It was difficult to contain the eagerness she felt at the

chance to work in a real laboratory for the first time in ages. She had absolutely no intention of spending any time away from her shiny new office, outside of mandatory interactions of course. Though the rooms in the tavern were probably quite lovely, Angela only ever felt at home when she was surrounded by the instruments of science.

At last, they rounded what was probably the only corner they hadn't turned in the entire settlement. The names and places Tomás had thrown at her were still spilling out of her head as the pair took the final steps from the town boardwalk toward the jetty that led to the research building. It was quite literally on the edge of town, isolated like a peninsula on the western border of the marsh, with open water -- not canals -- on all sides. But even knowing it was the most exposed building in the entire settlement did not stop her from wanting to burrow into it and make her own nest of paperwork, instruments, and research.

Tomás turned the key in the door, and she fought back a strained squeal of delight. It was small, but it was perfect.

Tinker Inn

Sometime later that evening, as the sun was beginning to sink below the treeline, Elias managed to coax Angela out of her nest to join the crew for a drink at the Tinker Inn.

"I'm telling you, El, the lab is perfect. I mean, it's nothing compared to how things were before, but it's so much more equipment than I've had in one place in a very long time."

"Well, I'm just happy you're happy," El said, skipping a rock into the murky water beside the causeway.

They walked along in comfortable silence for a while. Angela was no doubt thinking through organizational systems for the lab. Elias was taking in the scenery. Black clouds framed the fiery sky, and mosquitoes sang their evening song. Lamplighters trapsed up and down the boardwalk, chattering with each other and the shopkeepers closing up for the night. As they neared the tavern, Elias spoke up. "So, what are you helping these people with, anyhow? This place seems pretty self-sufficient."

Angela thought back to the letter Tomás had sent her and their conversation when he first brought her into the laboratory. "There's something strange going on at a nest near here. Remember how that bug just laid down and died, and then that other bug took its headgear?" She chewed her lip as she spoke. "Tomás seems to think we could go to their nest and find out what's making them sick, and then--"

Elias stopped in his tracks. "Wait, the man wants you to go *into* a living nest?"

Angela kept walking. "It's a little wacky, I know. But apparently, he's already been inside this one. And it won't be just me. Oar's Chapel is sending an escort."

"And how is a random laboratory considered adequate payment for *risking your life*? Can't they get what they need without you there?" He trotted to catch up with her.

"Well, I actually *want* to be there, El. Imagine going inside a *living* nest! A recon team mapped it all out for us a couple weeks ago. If I find out what's killing these bugs, we might be able to use it as a weapon against them. And, according to Tomás, we're going to try to harvest some of their tech. I have been *dying* to get my hands on an intact piece of that gear!"

They had arrived at the tavern. Angela made to step inside, but Elias grabbed her by the shoulders. "What happened to the Angela we all know and love? Hello, Dr. Practical? Are you in there?" He brought his face within a half inch of hers, staring deep into her eyes with a quizzical look. "*I'm* the adventurous, wistful one, remember? *You* are supposed to be science-y and serious!"

Angela laughed and shook her head, gently pushing her beloved companion off. "Maybe I'm a little star-struck by the lab. Maybe I'm batty from spending way too long in Draycott. Maybe I just need a second to not be so *safe* all the time ." She trailed off, the bitter tone of grief tinging her words. Everyone had lost so much in the years since the mega-bugs had landed. It was in those moments of safety when thoughts of danger and loss crept in and made the grief -- and the fear -- that much more bitter and pronounced.

El sought quickly to lighten the mood. "Or maybe it's just the funky air in this town?" As if on cue, the strange scent they smelled on the wind when they arrived that morning wafted past once more, this time mingled with alcohol from the tavern and the normal smells a settlement always has late in the evening. It was like flowers, but the nauseating kind. "We should get inside. The others are waiting for us."

The scene inside the tavern was alive with workers and townsfolk settling into the warmth of reverie. It was still too early for anyone to be very drunk, but by the looks of it, several parties were well on their way. Flighty, plucking notes of a banjo set the tone for the happy buzz of conversations and toasts, punctuated with laughter and the sloshing of alcohol from eclectic steins and stemware. The entire atmosphere of the tavern was *warm* and *safe*, as though the horrors of the outside world were just last night's bad dream.

Angela knew magickal places like this existed. She took great care not to allow herself to cross thresholds that led to them. But there was something so alluring about the atmosphere here, she found herself drawn in like a moth to a flame. Without hesitation, she entered, and the soft, warm glow of the tavern and its patrons enveloped her. She let the magick take her, just this once, to a time before everything bad had ever happened.

She took a seat at the bar and ordered something light. Elias followed suit. Beside them stood a short, spry fellow, balanced precariously on the swiveling bar stool. He swayed to and fro as he led the more inebriated parts of the tavern in a lively pub song. Angela and El watched, chiming in on the parts they could guess. After the final line, everyone took a swig of whatever drink they had in their hand.

The man standing on the chair chugged his entire stein, then plopped down haphazardly onto the stool and let out a bellowing belch. Angela could hardly stifle her laugh. He noticed and swiveled to look at her, giving a half-bow. "Marten McMurtry, at your service, milady!" Though endearing, the gesture was not elegant in the slightest, as he nearly tumbled off the stool mid-bow.

"Hi Marten. I'm Doctor Reyes, and this is Elias."

"How do you do! Wait... have we met before?!" He slurred every syllable, occasionally hiccuping between words.

"No, no, we just arrived today," Angela chuckled. "You seem to be enjoying yourself! Does the town gather like this every night?"

"Woah, woah -- *hic* -- woah, one question at a time, Doc! Doc... I called someone else Doc, once. Are you sure we haven't met?"

"Ange, let the man be. He's clearly drunk," Elias chimed in.

"No, no, a lady's company is rare these days. Let alone a doc-*hic*-tor! You folks came in at a good time. All here's in good spirits. In a few hours, this place will be a-brawlin'."

"Do you mean there will be fights tonight?" Angela asked, sipping her drink. It was quite bitter, watered-down stuff.

"There's fights most nights, Doc. We gather for camaraderie sometimes, but... well, hurting people hurt people. There-*hic* no such thing as a person ain't hurting these days." He paused and nursed the new beer that had arrived before him sometime after the pub song ended. It almost looked like he was done speaking at all until his glazed eyes lit up, and he nearly lept off the stool in excitement. "Doctor!"

"Yes?"

"No, I know the other doctor who passed through here a short time ago! Called him Doc, too!"

"Oh?" Angela knew there were others like her, traveling from place to place, helping settlements get on their feet, but she was under the impression she was the first of her kind to come by Furnmoss since the Arachnids arrived.

"Yes, ma'am! Doctor Van-something-er-other. I could never remember, just called him Doc. He went with Tomás to the nest near three months ago!"

"Oh, he did, did he?" Angela set her mug down with a frown. This was perplexing. Tomás had assured her she would be the first to have assessed the Arachnids at the Oar's Chapel nest.

"Yes, the poor soul." Marten lifted the stein in a silent toast and drank deeply.

Angela felt her stomach drop and the magick of the place tavern dwindled. "Poor soul?"

"May he rest in peace." Marten swallowed the last of his

beer, let out another belch, and started singing again, this time a lively tune about drinking to the dead.

Tomás had not lied to her, at least not directly. She was not the first scientist to pass through, but she *would* be the first to have game-changing information about the mega-bugs... *if* she made it back alive.

Swamp

It took the team two days to prepare for the journey out. Angela had yet to bring up the subject of the scientist who died on the last expedition. She wasn't sure she wanted to bring up something so bleak, especially with the mission approaching so quickly. Tomás had said the best time to go was during a monsoon and, according to the locals, a big storm was due any day. The team would have to be ready to leave at a moment's notice.

Sure enough, the wind picked up. A massive squall rolled toward them at thunderous speeds, sweeping in heavy, doom-filled clouds from the ocean. Rumbles of thunder and flashes of lightning heralded a storm that would last at least a week. As the team of ten made their way northwest into the swamp, the people of Furnmoss battened down the hatches in preparation for this, the first of many spring storms to come.

The road to the nest took the team five miserable, unbelievably muddy days on foot. Far away from the beaten path, they found themselves carving out their own trail, sometimes having to double back in places where the foliage grew too dense to fight through. All the while, rain assailed them from the heavens in unrelenting sheets. Layers of clouds hung oppressively above the dense canopy, suffocating the sunlight.

Everyone and everything was soaked to the bone. It took three days for Angela to reach her limit. Everything in her wanted to turn back. Tired, sore, and quite put off at the prospect of having another soggy, tasteless ration for dinner at the end of the night, she fought her way to the head of the pack, where Tomás was breaking trail. She struggled to get a word in as he hacked into a particularly stubborn patch of branches with his machete. At last, he stopped to catch his breath and declared that they must reroute yet again.

"Tomás," she began, "I know you've been through here before. I know about the other scientist. Why can't we use the trail you took with him?"

Tomás squatted against a tree stump, his sweat mixing with the rain and the mud. "Because, Doctor Reyes, that path can only be traversed in the dry season. At the moment, it's underwater."

"So... why are we doing *this*," she gestured to the overall ickiness of the current situation, "when there's an easier, drier way? Shouldn't we just wait for the rain to clear up and try again when it's not so awful?" Even as she spoke, she could feel the mud sucking her boots in deeper. It was like the swamp was trying to eat her alive. She hated it.

Tomás paused, took a sip from his canteen, and sighed. "The bugs don't travel in weather like this. We haven't seen any living bugs for days, not in the air, not on the ground, because if they try to fly, the lightning gets 'em, and if they try to walk, they become part of the swamp soup. I know you are uncomfortable, Doctor Reyes; we all are. But I assure you, it's safer this way." He sighed, his tired face twisted with grief and frustration. "Last time we tried this, we were arrogant and unprepared. We lost that scientist and several other good men because of that, and I won't have it happen again. This is the path the recon team said they took, but it seems the foliage grew back twice as thick where they cut it out. I'm sorry, but it really is the best we've got."

"I understand." This was the price she had to pay. *A few more days,* she reminded herself.

It was three days, to be precise. Three more days of mushy, yet somehow also stale, rations. Three more days of forging a path through the god-forsaken swamp. Three more days of unsticking herself from the muck each morning, exhausted from yet another night of restless sleep amidst the downpour. But each day brought them closer to the mound in the distance that was the Arachnid's nest. Closer to knowledge. Closer to revenge.

When they finally arrived, the stench that had drifted subtly around Furnmoss finally hit them in its purest form. It had been growing almost undetected on the undercurrent of the air they breathed as they approached the place, but now it was practically impossible to ignore. It was floral, mixed with the rot of decaying flesh and the sour stench of acidweb. There was something more to it, though Angela could not quite pick out what it was. The closest descriptor she could find was *yeasty*, but not in the pleasing way of fresh-baked bread. They made camp for the night on the edge of the clearing where the massive nest stood.

As sunrise lit the clouds an ominous green, the team carefully traversed the minefield of acidweb, dilapidated egg sacs, and very old carcasses surrounding the mound. Sometime close to midday, they reached the foot of the hill, and Tomás led them to a crevice just wide enough to fit a person. Two guards planted themselves outside while the rest of the crew made their way into the dark.

The temperature dropped sharply in the dank cool of the cave. Still sopping wet, the crew stifled shivers as they squeezed into the moist, tight space. As they went, the way somehow became even more narrow. The ceiling sank closer and closer to the floor of the cave. At one point, about twenty minutes in, the crew had to drop to their hands and knees to continue, and eventually down to their bellies. The damp walls cradled every part of their bodies as they kicked and thrust their way inward and downward toward the chilling draft and purple-ish glow of the dank inside of the nest.

Just as the tunnel became almost too tight to traverse, it released its grip, opening to a small cavern. The space was just big enough to fit their eight-person team – if they pretended they were a can of sardines. Surrounded entirely by densely-packed mud walls, the only way out of the cavern was through a porthole, about seven feet off the ground and four feet in diameter. One by one, Tomás hoisted the team up, and they pulled themselves through the hole.

At last, it was Angela's turn. Her tired body had found a reserve of adrenaline, and her heart thumped hard in her chest. She had no idea what to expect on the other side of the porthole. She glanced at Tomás, who was braced against the wall and waiting for her to climb up.

"What if they see us?" she asked, wringing her cold hands.

"Most of them should be resting right now to conserve energy for the hunt after the rain lets up. They have occasional patrols, but I don't think they expect anyone to make it this far in. Besides, they have other things to worry about right now. The recon team said there were rooms and rooms of quarantined sick ones. According to them, it looked like the healthy ones were busy keeping the nest."

Angela nodded. Her question was still unanswered. "So... if they see us?"

Tomás laughed. "If they see us, start running."

Angela laughed, partly because she was nervous and partly because that really was the only correct answer, even if it was obvious and useless. She thought of Elias' very valid objections to this dangerous endeavor and sighed, trying to muster up the same courage that had led her here in the first place. No, not courage. Stupidity. It was definitely stupidity. But she was here now, and backing out would be just as senseless as going forward. "In the name of science, then."

"Whatever helps you sleep at night, Doc. Make sure Mac up there remembers to pull me up before he goes on looking for scrap."

"Will do." She put her foot in his interlocked palms and stepped up. As she pulled herself up and out through the slippery canal, she entered at ground level, like a mouse through a hole in the wall of a mansion.

Nest

It was dizzying to come from such a cramped tunnel into a room the size of an airplane hangar. Angela leaned her back against the wall to take in the magnificent architecture inside. Above them towered a domed ceiling, buttresses and arches and pillars of dirt holding the structure up in an unexpectedly elegant fashion. To either side were myriad corridors that probably lead to even more rooms just like this one. Mac hoisted Tomás through the hole, and the eight stood there momentarily to catch their bearings. Tomás pulled out the map of the inside of the nest, and they huddled together.

Tomás handed out pocket notebooks and pens to each person, then addressed them all in a whisper. "Okay, everyone, it's just like we planned. There's a map in each of these notebooks. Use it to find your marks. Take notes on what you see. Draw pictures if there's time. Mac and Laura, you'll be headed to the rooms colored purple to scavenge for tech. Angela and I are going to the quarantined areas, in red, to gather samples. Garrett, Bert, do the same with the nurseries. They're colored green. We'll meet back here in thirty minutes. Everyone clear?" There were nods of agreement all around, and the team split up.

About three minutes into their trek down one corridor, Angela spotted an Arachnid. She and Tomás squatted behind a pile of dirt, watching as the creature approached. Angela held her breath, observing from behind the pile. She was surprised to see Tomás leaning out toward the beast in an attempt to observe it.

"Doc," he whispered, "C'mere, look at this one. It's got no eyes."

"It's *what*?" She peeked up from the hiding place to see the rather short, stout mega-bug as it passed them.

Sure enough, it had no eyes, and no purple-lit augmentation on its head, either. Instead, its pedipalps were replaced with piston-powered shovel-like tools, connected to a whirring, blinking machine that rested on its cephalothorax where eyes would have been. The machine had some extended, bulky mechanism that draped over the creature's abdomen. From it, sprawled valves attached to more pistons plugged into the bug's back legs. It tromped past them, pistons hissing as it walked. It seemed to be completely unaware of their presence. Angela furiously scribbled in her notebook until it rounded the corner of the corridor, and the pair continued on their way to the quarantine rooms.

The scene was dismal. The group came upon a room that was clearly a converted nursery. Groups of sickly, weak-looking Arachnids of all shapes, sizes, and types huddled together amidst infection-ridden egg sacs. A thick layer of orange-ish dust was slathered on the walls, the bugs, and the egg sacs.

In one corner of the room was a pile of carcasses, some Arachnid, some human, some indistinguishable. The orange stuff was everywhere. One sightless Arachnid was working to remove tech from the dead bugs. The pile of deceased was leaning up against a tall spire of some sort, topped with a dangling, round, white-ish bulb. Were these sacrifices? Offerings?

"Tell me what you need, Doc," said Tomás.

"If I can get a piece of that infected egg sac, we're in business." For a moment, she wondered if whatever was killing the bugs was contagious to humans. She hadn't considered it, but what if it was airborne? She reached into her pocket and found a too-wet bandana to tie around her nose and mouth.

"We're not robbing a train, Doc."

"We might be susceptible to whatever they have. It's just a precaution."

"Right." Tomás pulled down the mosquito net on his hat and tucked it into his collar.

"Those eggs right there on the edge of it should be easy to reach if we can just find a distraction."

"They're sick; they shouldn't have the energy to come after us," offered Tomás before stepping out to test his theory. Angela hesitantly followed, but as they neared the patch of ruined egg sacs, there was a commotion at a nearby cluster of the quarantined Arachnids.

With a screech, one of the Arachnids charged toward them from the center of the room. Or at least it seemed to be charging at them. Tomás and Angela ducked behind the meter-high egg sacs, and instead of following them, the creature made for the exit. It reached the corridor, a puff of orange dust floating in the air behind it. But just as it crossed the threshold, another Arachnid rushed in from the hallway and tackled the first one to the ground. The two tussled, garnering clicks and squeals from the quarantined creatures.

Amidst the ruckus, Angela gathered a respectably large sample of egg sac lining, two quarts of the viscous slime from inside the egg sac, and a small spiderling egg that had not hatched. She sealed the samples in plastic and shoved them into her pack, then grabbed Tomás and pulled him toward the door as the two battling Arachnids tumbled toward the quarantined group of mega-bugs, throwing clouds of ocher orange into the air.

The scientist examined the egg sac lining as the pair waited in the small cavern attached to their escape route. Everything they had collected was covered in that orange dust. She and Tomás were covered in it, too.

"Perhaps it's a medicine." she wondered aloud before removing her bandana and sniffing a bit of it that had settled on her sleeve. She gave a quick sneeze before registering the smell. It was nauseatingly floral, like how the old cleaning supplies used to try to replicate natural scents. And it was one more thing.... It was *yeasty*.

"You think they're using that stuff to heal their sick?" Tomás asked.

"If they are, it isn't working very well." She pulled out

her notebook to sketch some sights she'd seen as they waited for the rest of the team to return.

The journey back was as grueling as the journey there, but the team's morale had greatly improved. Their return trip was littered with excited retellings of all the things the explorers had encountered. According to Mac and Laura, who had pilfered almost more tech than the group could carry back, there were entire store rooms filled with tech. Most of it looked older, damaged, dirty. Most of it was covered in the same orange dust Angela and Tomás had seen in the quarantine room.

"I think," said Laura, "they take it off the dead, clean it up, and attach it to the spiderlings once they hatch."

"Did you see how many types there were?" Garrett asked, remarking on the rows and rows of egg sacs that lined the nursery floors and walls. "Someone has to lay all those eggs. One of these days, we'll find out where they keep the queen."

"I just hope this will all lead to an era of great change for humanity," Angela said as the gates of Furnmoss came into view.

"We're going to turn the table on those Arachnid bastards, for sure," Tomás said, and the team cheered in agreement.

The merry party returned to Furnmoss, eager to share their findings with the good citizens of Oar's Chapel, and, eventually, the world. And the team's findings would most certainly change the world, though not in the way they had hoped.

Ground Zero

Back at the lab, Angela was hard at work studying the samples the team had collected. Early that morning, she'd sent out a courier with a letter to her dear friend, a microbiologist by the name of Maruis LaPorte, who she was confident could help her identify what was causing the Oar's Chapel Phenomenon. She knew he rarely left his post at Hillfar Fastness, but she had a hunch that once he read her letter, he would leave for Furnmoss with a quickness.

Between tests on pieces of the samples she'd collected, Angela went to check on the tech the team had recovered, which she quarantined in an air-tight observation chamber. In total, there were twelve pieces. Wait. not twelve. Thirteen. There were *thirteen* pieces in all, and one had gone missing. Immediately she thought back to Tomás. On her first day in Furnmoss, as he showed her around the university lab, he told her of his plan to sell the tech they salvaged to other towns in Oar's Chapel. She threw her clipboard onto the counter with an annoyed grunt and donned her rain gear.

Her arrival at the Tinker Inn, where Tomás was tending bar for the day, took the governor by surprise. Still, he seemed happy to see her. "Doc! I thought you'd be in that lab a few more days before you returned to my little tavern!"

Angela had no time for niceties. "What did you do with the tech you took from my lab? It was supposed to stay there, quarantined until Doctor LaPorte okayed it."

Tomás sighed and leaned on the counter. "Look, Doc, I figure if any of that Arachnid stuff was contagious, we'd know by now. You, me, the team? We all went *into* the nest. Wouldn't we be sick if humans could catch it? I don't know about you, but I'm feelin' healthy as a winning horse on race day!"

"Where is it, Tomás?"

Exasperated, he went back to wiping down the bar counter. "I sent it out to the governor of Listinglass."

"You *what?*"

"Yeah, he didn't believe me that we went into the nest and got a bunch of gear, but he said if I could prove I had it he'd put in an offer to buy half of it." He shrugged. "I sent it as a gesture of good faith."

Angela was speechless. Her jaw clenched so tight she thought it might break. How could someone be so careless?

"Doc, none of us is sick. It didn't even look dirty! Now, in case you didn't know, we're having a festival tonight to celebrate all our hard work. Town's got a parade set up. They're putting out decorations as we speak. Maybe you could cut loose tonight, have a drink, dance with your buddy Elias, and just enjoy the atmosphere. You've been working since you got here."

There was no stopping the courier he'd sent, who would likely arrive at Listinglass in a few hours. Angela sighed, unscrewed her jaw, and forced a tight smile. "Sure thing, Tomás. We'll be there tonight."

As part of her preparations for the festival that night, she sent out a courier to warn Listinglass of the potential danger that tech posed to their much smaller town. She donned her dressiest pair of pants and her most colorful shirt and walked with Elias down to the center of Furnmoss.

The parade and the drinking had already begun, and the pair soon joined the rest of Furnmoss in exuberant revelry. At the end of the parade route was an enormous feast, tables lined up in the middle of the road, and a stage with a massive table where the team who had infiltrated the

Oar's Chapel nest had the honor of sitting and sharing stories as they all ate and drank to their hearts' content.

But even as she felt herself unwind, and as the sun sank low and the stars poked through drizzling clouds, and the festival grew rowdy, Angela knew something was not quite right. She imagined she could see traces of orange dust in the damp night air. Eventually, as the celebration continued on into the wee hours of the morning, she managed to push the anxiety from her mind. Between dancing, storytelling, drinking, and dining, she had even found herself in the arms of a beautiful woman with an "eel farm," whatever that was, on the edge of town.

And somewhere along the way, Angela fell into a deep, intoxicated sleep. Images of dancing Arachnids and dinner tables coated in ocher dust plagued her dreams, mixed with the baleful cries and aching groans of invisible people dying slow, painful deaths.

Except the screams were real.

She awoke to them, at first thinking she'd merely nodded off while the party was in full swing. But as she sat up in her chair on the stage, she could see a pale orange haze mingling with the morning fog. It settled on her skin, staining it despite her best efforts to scrub it off with her sleeve. It itched, like her skin was crawling with millions of tiny little bugs. As the world around her came painfully into view, she saw the boardwalk through the throbbing of her hangover. All that had once been a faded, waterlogged brown was now colored an unsettling ocher, and the canal streets were layered in a thickening froth of brownish-orange slime.

And the people...

Laying about, some on the street, some in their dinghies, some in their chairs, were the people of Furnmoss, all painted in a sickly orange, just like her. She could hear screams in the distance, guttural gurgling from somewhere nearby, anxious prayers unceasing from hopeless, babbling mouths. Pushing through her malaise, she made her way toward the lab. As she went, she could see tall figures looming in the fog of various boardwalks where the wails and mutterings of concerned citizens echoed.

She wanted to investigate -- she *needed* to investigate -- but first, she needed to send out a note to Marius to let him know not to come here without proper protection. To tell him the ocher dust was *invading* the town of Furnmoss like a plague.

At last, she reached the lab. To her dismay, the door had been opened by some unknown intruder, and out from the opening sprawled orange and white tendrils, like tentacles or roots, gripping the walls of the place. Cautiously, she entered. Her stomach lurched with regret from the night before and sank in terror at what was inside.

The body lay sprawled and spasming on the lab floor beside a broken bottle of liquor. Such a sight would be harrowing enough, but that was not the worst part. Angela reached down to hold his hand as it scraped at the floor, blood sticking to his fingers and the linoleum tile. A stuttering sob escaped her throat and whispered, "Elias, it's me."

He whimpered in reply. He maybe even tried to speak. But the garbled noise was nonsense beneath the weight of the full stalk of the massive, orange fungus that grew out of his mouth. The weight of it had shattered his jaw and pulled it so far to the right that his tongue and mandible lolled to the side, plastered to the floor by the thing's sticky tendrils. Suddenly, his blood-rimmed eyes bugged out in pain as the thing seemed to shiver, then grow in diameter and height by a good few centimeters. There was the cracking of bone and a pleading, garbled cry before he passed out.

Angela knew what she needed to do. She needed to help Elias, who she could not save, and then she needed to try and save the town. She steeled herself, grabbed the firearm she kept hidden under her pillow, and said a prayer over Elias before taking care of him in the only way she could. When the bullet left the gun, the fungus flailed erratically, shaking from its tentacles to its bulbous head. As it shook, it threw small orange particles into the air. Then, the tip of it shot up straight, and, with a quivering *pop!* it exploded, ocher spores pouring out all over the lab and the dock outside.

Doctor Angela Reyes struggled to breathe through the orange miasma that clung to the fog as she wrote her final letter to Doctor Marius LaPorte. She could feel something take root in her chest as she roamed the streets and tried to help the townspeople. When she realized nothing was to be done out there, she retired to her lab to study spore samples, hoping against hope to find something to destroy the infestation. Outside, the citizens lit their homes on fire and cleansed themselves with astringent and expired household chemicals from days past. They even threw kerosene on the stalks, but their efforts were simply not enough to quash the fungal spread.

Somewhere east of Oar's Chapel, a courier pushed his steed to the limit. Doctor Reyes had sent him with very specific instructions.

"First and foremost, don't stop until you get there. Not for food, not for water, not for sleep. Second, don't let anyone get close. If you see anyone on the road, steer clear of them. Finally, keep the letter on your person, but when you arrive at the gate, deliver what it says by mouth, far from the entrance, far from people. Tell them Angela sent you with an urgent message for Marius, but you're contagious and can't come inside. If they don't listen to you, *make them*."

But even as his horse died beneath him, and he doggedly pushed forward on foot, the courier could feel the sharp pain of something pushing hard from the inside of the bridge of his nose. He trudged on, powered forward by the horrific scenes of tall fungi growing on the boardwalks of Furnmoss, crippling the bodies of his people. But his muscles grew tired. A general feeling of malaise settled over him, accompanying the dizzying pain in his face. Still, he continued toward Hillfar Fastness.

Were the courier's blood under a microscope, one might see the fungal cells mingling with it, drinking it up like soup as they combined and divided and grew into something more powerful. Even as he pushed onward, the growing tendrils of the fungus wove themselves into the muscles of his arms and legs, making him stiff, forcing him to slow, then crawl, then drag himself until every tiny twitch and spasm of movement was excruciating.

The fungus let him breathe, let him think, let him see. And when at last all he could do was lie there, he was somehow, miraculously compelled to turn onto his back and look up at the sky. For a moment, he felt peace. He watched the clouds roll by. He breathed in the sweetness of the earth after rainfall. He dozed a while in the warm afternoon sun. He even dreamed of his mother, now likely victim to his same fate, baking pastries back home at Furnmoss.

The pain of the fungus pushing forward through the center of his face, tendrils sprawling out from it to plaster him to the ground, was enough to end him. His body would stay alive, the fungus needed the sustenance, but his person was broken beyond repair. The last thing he saw, as the massive stalk grew, and grew, and grew, was the glitter of midnight stars. The last thing he heard would come much, much later. Amidst the unpleasant darkness of the fungus, and the putrid scent of his own body decaying, and the delirium of malnutrition and pain, came the slow, building rumble of hoofbeats and wagon wheels on the ground.

4

GALINA

CW HAWES

GALINA PAUSED for a moment and looked at the giant airship. The lights on the airstrip barely illuminated the black hull. Two hundred and twenty-seven meters long, the nineteen gas cells held more than sixty-eight thousand cubic meters of hydrogen gas. The five engines enabled a cruising speed of one hundred and five kilometers per hour. This was a beautiful ship. The best in the fleet. And she was proud she'd made the cut to serve on her.

She took a deep breath and exhaled. She was eighteen years old and this was her eighteenth mission. She was a survivor, for few airshipmen made it beyond ten missions. And those who did shared a special camaraderie.

A hand slapped her shoulder. "You going to stare at her all night, or are you coming on board?"

Dimitri, the starboard gunner. The best in the fleet. "In a minute," she answered.

"Don't wait too long." He held up a hip flask. "Or no vodka for you!"

She waved him away and watched him trot to the ship.

The bugs were cunning and powerful adversaries. It

took good gunners to keep them away from the ships. It also took a good captain who knew his ship well and could fly her into and out of danger, and Captain Tolonovski was the best. This was her fifth mission on the D19, and she had nothing but high regard for her captain. Good men and women served on this ship, and she was proud to serve with them. For the glory of the Motherland, and the death of the bugs.

A smile touched her lips. With a little bit of luck she'd return home a hero. A Defender of the Motherland. For this was a special mission, they'd been told. One that promised, if successful, to spell the end of the bugs.

She watched the experimental bombs being loaded into the bomb bay. Two one-tonne bombs that carried a special formulation of the parasitic fungus that was the bane of bugs and humans alike. The fungus would destroy the bugs and rid the earth of them forever. Life would go back to the way it was in the Before Time. The time prior to the arrival of the giant spider-like aliens.

The alarm sounded and brought Galina out of her revery. She trotted to the giant airship and climbed aboard, greeting her fellow crew members, and saluting the officers.

She made her way aft and climbed the twenty-four meters to her spot on the top of the ship near the giant tailfin. She patted the 13mm Borovski heavy machine gun, donned her helmet and parka, and prepared the gun for action.

The sun had set a half hour ago. Flying the giant airships at night helped to avoid superheating of the lift gas, which would cause it to be valved off. It was tactically important to have as much lift gas as possible in the giant cells.

Through the helmet's headphones she heard the

captain give the command, "Up ship!", and slowly the glow from the ground lights disappeared, leaving only the dusky darkness, and the millions of pinpoints of starlight dotting the night sky.

In the distance, on either side of the D19 were the other ships in the bombing squadron. Visible only due to the faint glow of the lights in the command gondolas.

Once again she heard the captain's voice through her headphones: "Engines ahead three-quarters. Up elevators five degrees." She felt the ship angle upward and begin its climb to its cruising altitude of five thousand meters. Such an extreme altitude was necessary to avoid the flyers for as long as possible.

The minutes slipped by and the squadron drew closer to its target, the giant arachnid nest some two hundred kilometers northwest of the base. Nicknamed Arachnograd 7.

Galina sucked on her oxygen bottle. Her eyes peered through the night vision goggles and carefully searched the sky for bugs. The flyers were black as night, and it was only by catching either their form blotting out stars, or the glint of light from their technological enhancements that one knew they were there.

The air was bitingly cold. Frost covered everything. Her machine gun was white with the stuff. Each time she exhaled, she added to the accumulation. She slapped her gloved hands together to keep the feeling in them. More than ever she wished she could take a swig from Dimitri's hip flask and feel the burning warmth of the vodka.

The night sky was beautiful. The stars were brilliant. There were no clouds to obscure them. No moon to outshine them. But Galina paid little attention to the dramatic display. Watching for flyers was far more important then admiring the beauty of nature.

Her mind drifted to the stories told by the Elders of her city, how the bugs just appeared one day. Their spaceships hovered over all the big cities of earth. At first, the people were in awe. There was hope for a partnership with the aliens, a peaceful exchange of ideas and technology. But when the invasion began, everyone immediately realized the bugs had come for one simple reason. They were hungry.

Those early days, the Elders said, were horrible beyond description. The giant, hairy, black things slaughtered and ate everything that moved. And while the fat ground bugs were extremely deadly, the more slender flyers were even worse. They covered more territory and did it faster and prepared the area for the ground bugs to move in. If there was anything alive, it didn't live for long.

Galina shook her head. No time for stories. There were flyers out there. Waiting for them. She just knew it, and continued to scan the inky sky.

She felt the airship begin its descent for the bombing run, which was the most dangerous part of the mission. For the bombs to have the best chance of hitting the target, the ship had to be below fifteen hundred meters. And that meant fighting off the flyers. Which wasn't always successful.

They could cling to the airship hull with their padded feet and pick off the gunners, leaving the ship defenseless. They could shoot poison web and dissolve large parts of the ship, ruining the aerodynamics and causing a crash. Their cutting mandibles could shear through the girders and beams. But if they were hit with13mm armor-piercing rounds, the bugs didn't stand a chance. Galina smiled. During her previous missions, she'd made certain that hundreds of the monstrosities hadn't returned to their nests.

She studied the night sky on either side of the giant tailfin. Nothing but stars and the inky blackness. She slowly rotated the gun mount until it was facing forward. The frigid wind blasted her face, and she quickly rotated the gun mount so she was once again looking aft.

Let Kirill deal with the wind. Poor devil. The bow gunner was the worst position on the airship.

She pulled the furs tighter. The freezing altitude, coupled with the ninety-seven kph slipstream, made hypothermia a very real possibility. She slapped her hands together and slapped her shoulders, all the while keeping a watchful eye for the enemy.

She thought again of the briefing session the captain gave before they'd boarded the ship. This mission was probably the most important mission she would ever fly. If successful, it would spell the end of the bugs. Galina could not imagine what life would be like without them. It was all she knew. Bugs and the fear of bugs. But she hoped the scientists were right.

The most brilliant minds of the Motherland had made a super weapon out of the fungus, which had appeared as mysteriously as had the bugs. Though the fungus attacked people and bugs indiscriminately, it was the most effective bug killer on the planet.

The crew hadn't been told much, and she understood little of what they had been told. But it seemed that the main part of the fungus was the part that grew in the bodies of the bugs and people. The mushroom was the fruiting part. Kind of like an apple blossom, only far more ugly and dangerous.

The bombs contained enough modified spores to infect the entire bug nest. The spores would develop into the parasitic mycelium and kill the bugs, but would not produce fruiting bodies. They'd kill the host and then die. No more need for scrubbers to come in after a battle to kill the mushrooms, or to follow the troops when they stormed a nest that had been bombed.

The klaxon sounded, and she heard the call, "Battle stations. All hands, battle stations." Flyers had been sighted. Now came the test of wills.

Galina rotated the gun mount to starboard. In the distance, she saw gunfire. The D15 was under attack. The airship was too far away to make out the details. The muzzle flashes and tracers from the machine guns lit up the night.

She slowly swung the gun to the port, eyes sweeping the sky. Ahead, she saw muzzle flashes from the D17. And then she saw the stars disappear. Flyers coming in. She pulled back the cocking lever, aimed, and squeezed the trigger.

The roar of the machine gun was deafening. The muzzle flash almost blinding. She watched the tracers, adjusted her aim, and was rewarded with a screech. A hit. The bug plummeted to earth.

No time to gloat. Another bug was swooping in, heading for the tail. She had to get it before it spit poison web and destroyed the ship's rudder.

She pulled the trigger, and watched where the armor-piercing bullets ripped into the thing. The thorax blew apart, its legs curled up, and the thing fell to earth.

Bullets whizzed past her. *What the hell?* She rotated the gun mount in time to see a bug slide off the hull. Kirill had saved her life, and now the poor devil was surrounded by flyers.

She opened fire. The bullets ripped apart the bugs swarming her fellow gunner. Legs, wings, chunks of exoskeleton flew through the air. And then Kirill's gun went silent. The tell-tale sign of poison web.

The giant spider-like aliens were swarming the ship and were so numerous no stars could be seen. It was as if they knew the airship carried their doom, their extinction from the world they thought they'd conquered.

Galina saw a shape coming towards her from the bow. Her machine gun spewed death. She watched the armor piercing rounds smash into the thing's head. Mouth parts and Arachnid techno-devices sprayed out from the alien's body. The macerated remains hit the hull and slid off, just missing taking Galina's gun mount with them.

She swung the gun around and dealt death to another flyer. She pulled the trigger. Nothing. The ammo box was empty. She opened a new one and fed in the belt.

A bug dropped onto the hull right in front of her. The thing's furry palps rubbed together. She saw poison drip from the fangs. The stench was nauseating. Her hand reached down and grabbed the shotgun next to her seat. She brought it up as the front legs reached for her, and pumped two armor piercing slugs into the beast's face.

It lurched backwards. The legs curled up, and it slid off the hull.

Another flyer landed near the tailfin. She closed the loading gate, pulled back on the cocking lever, and squeezed the trigger. The bug blew apart, but it was too late. She watched the upper tailfin dissolve beneath the coating of poison web.

This was not good. The ship might be able to make the flight home with just the lower rudder, and if anyone could make that flight, it was Captain Tolonovski, but would he be able to get the ship out of the heat of battle intact enough to make the flight?

The ship shuddered, and she felt that feeling of weightlessness. The ship was dropping. Something was wrong. Had the bugs made it on board? Had they cut their way through the girders?

There was nothing from the gondola. All around her was the sound of gunfire. Another bug came swooping in and Galina pulled the trigger. The beast hit the hull, tore the fabric, and went over the side.

Suddenly the ship shot upwards. This too was not a good sign. Only once before had she been on such a ride in an airship, and that was when her ship had gotten caught in a storm. But here, in this situation? She could smell her own fear.

Did the captain drop all their ballast? Maybe he released the bombs. He might have done either or both to keep the ship afloat. Maybe that is what happened.

For an eternity, the airship hung in the sky. There were no flyers. The ship had gone higher than they could fly. Galina saw the stars, the constellations and the stories they told. Yes, they were beautiful.

And then she felt the bottom fall out of the world. The tail dropped, and the airship began plummeting towards the earth.

In horror, Galina watched the ground rushing towards her. She saw a pale yellow luminescence spreading and illuminating the night. Were those the new spores? The bug killers?

There was nothing but the glowing earth rushing up to meet her. This was it.

"I hope we won and my death is swift. Glory to the Motherland," she said.

Moments later, the airship slammed into the earth.

End

5

ICHOR SUMMER

JB LETTERCAST

Scrubber

Elvan Solak looked out across the field of bodies before him. It spanned from horizon to horizon. Pops of color poked out here and there, resembling a stained glass mosaic. To his left was unmistakable purple of Arachnid blood. It leached from those unfortunate ones led into battle against their will. Iridescent green glinted in the sun as a drone's disembodied wing shifted stiffly in the breeze. A long, black, hairy appendage stuck straight out of the ground like a decapitated tree with shaggy bark. There were pale pinks, dark browns, blobs of pasty white and muted gray, trails of that unique, deep, visually sticky kind of red that only humans can leave. All these colors came together in a sort of kaleidoscope collage of carnage.

This was Elvan's life, because, amidst the blender of bloating bellies, detached thoraces, and still-wet-bone, the unmistakable orange of the fungus would spread. And ever since humans had engineered the fungus into a weapon, it spread several hundred times faster than its original form.

Even as he took in the view, the fungus swallowed all those distinct splotches of color he'd seen only moments ago. He and the other scrubbers were there to keep the threat contained, weed it out so the battlefield could be cleared and used for infrastructure, and hopefully not die in the process. The fungus moved so quickly that the scrubbers had to start cleaning before the battle was even over. In the distance, he could hear the report of weapons. He could feel the *thump thump thump* of them in his chest.

Crrraaack!

The sound of yet another fungus bud sprouting through the cranium of the nearest carcass pulled Elvan Solak from his reverie. On instinct, he pumped the valve for the canister of herbicide on his back. He didn't need to aim. With one squeeze of the trigger and a sweeping motion, he sealed his foe's fate. Fat, heavy droplets of the poison dispersed from his sprayer, mingling with the pink and orange mist of viscera and spores that tinted the air. He whispered a prayer as the vile stuff hit the bud and the corpse housing it. The fungus wobbled and shriveled in rapid decay, and the skin of the soldier's demolished face bubbled, melted, and peeled. He paused to watch and see that the man wasn't still alive before moving on.

More times than he wished to consider, the bodies he sprayed were still alive in one sense or another. Their already painful death-by-fungus would be amplified to the *n*th degree the moment the poison made contact. Every few sprays or so, an unfortunate scrubber was tasked with using a captive bolt stunning gun to end that nightmare for another unlucky soldier. It's nearly impossible to forget the inhuman gurgling screams that erupt out of a faceless warrior as their body is invaded by fungus and their skin is melted down by a highly toxic and very deadly fungicide.

The recoil of the captive bolt gun as it *squelches* into exposed brain matter is equally haunting.

Luckily, the shriveling corpse he'd just cleared showed no notable signs of life, so he stepped over it in pursuit of another sprouting bud -- and nearly lost his footing as the ground rocked and the carpet of corpses shifted beneath him. The vibration could have been a natural earthquake or an earth-shaker bomb beneath the battlefield; he had no idea how to tell the difference. Regardless, he landed on his hands and knees and felt the familiar tug and restricted airflow of a tangled respirator hose. Mindfully, he reached around his breathing apparatus and found the snag. With a deft flick of his wrist, the hose loosened, and he sat back on his heels to drink in the revived flow of clean air. Somewhere nearby, there was a shout for the scrubbers to pick up the pace. He sighed, stood, and continued onward.

Farmer

In another life, Elvan would have been a wealthy farmer. Born in Northpass just a generation after the Arachnids arrived on Earth, his whole early life was centered around learning how to live off the land, weather the elements, and, most importantly, how to stave off the Arachnids. He lived on a large plot of farmland with his parents, grandparents, thirteen siblings, and all the livestock and crops they had cultivated as a community.

Much of the growing population of Northpass was related to his family in some way or another. Many by marriage, some by blood, others by business contract. Over time, the settlement became a safe harbor for those passing through, a dream destination for anyone wanting to grow a family. The land was fertile, the air was too dry for the fungus to take hold, and the nearest Arachnid nest was almost fifteen miles away.

From the moment he became a big brother, Elvan dutifully followed the path laid out for him as the eldest son in his family, but that all changed once the soldiers arrived. They claimed to be seeking asylum from the violent city-state of Truydan; they stood accused of cowardice for refusing to torture prisoners of war. Against all odds, on the night before their execution -- and Truydani-executions were lengthy, violent acts -- the soldiers had escaped their jail cells during a particularly damaging Arachnid attack on their encampment.

When they finally reached the bustling settlement of Northpass, they were on the verge of starvation and had lost half their party. The townsfolk took them in, fed them, and gave them jobs. Within a week, there were more Truydani soldiers at the gate seeking recompense. But they wanted more than the simple return of their criminals -- they were there to claim any and all people dwelling in Northpass as new citizens of the expanding city-state of Truydan.

There was no offer of diplomacy, no meeting of leaders in the interest of peace, only a demand for surrender – or else, oblivion. The people of Northpass were prepared to fight off Arachnids and small bands of raiders, but they had never faced an army like this. Still, they refused to surrender and even managed to hold their ground for about ten days. But their people were dying, the walls were crumbling, and all the noise had attracted the interest of the Arachnids.

Elvan was twelve years old when he became the patriarch of his family. He would never forget his father's face as he gathered and led the remaining able-bodied citizens of Northpass in a last-ditch effort to buck the

Truydani siege. He would never forget his mother's screams as she watched the resulting massacre from their rooftop or her haunted eyes as she told him to take his siblings and make a run for it. It was the last day he saw anyone in his family. It was the day he became a man.

As he and his brothers and sisters raced for the drainage pipe at the lowest point in the settlement, he would hear the sound of their eastern wall being reduced to rubble. He would hear the cries of his people as they were captured and dragged to cages waiting just outside the gates. Even through all the chaos, he managed to get all his siblings into the drainage pipe. As he lowered the youngest down to the second oldest, he locked eyes with a soldier who promptly made a beeline for their position.

"Run!" He shouted into the dark hole, then pulled the grate back over the top of it just in time for the man to grab him by the shirt and fling him into the air. He hit the ground on his back with a heavy thud and rolled to his side, gasping for breath.

The soldier grabbed him again in the same fashion as before, this time throwing him over his shoulder like a shepherd would a lost lamb. "This will go smoother if you don't fight, kid," the soldier's low rumbling voice carried from behind his ghoulish battlemask.

Elvan was still too breathless to respond. All that came out were sobbing gasps.

"I won't tell anyone about your family in the sewer. I can't promise they'll be safe. I can't promise you'll be safe either," he paused to shoot a Northpass man dead.

Elvan knew that dead man. It was Garrett. Garrett was betrothed to Elvan's oldest sister, and now Elvan was watching the life drain from his eyes. Garrett mouthed something as he watched the soldier carry Elvan out the city gates, and then he was gone. They were both gone. Garrett was gone into the arms of death, and Elvan was gone into the jaws of the enemy. Plumes of smoke poured out of the demolished town of Northpass, and the cages outside the gate were crammed full of people. But his mother was not there.

Elvan had the sense that anyone left inside the town would not survive. But were the people in the cages any safer from harm? Somehow it was louder out here, outside the town. A few yards beyond the cages, a team of Truydani soldiers expertly fought off a small squad of Arachnids. He could hear cries of men and women alike coming from all around. He could hear the thrusting of swords and the echo of gunfire. In the distance, he could almost make out the sound of his own name on the wind, but no matter how hard he listened, he could not be certain the call was for him. The noise of battle overwhelmed him, and he shut his eyes tight.

Prisoner

He was curled up on a cot when he awoke. His back hurt. The room was swaying. The ground was bouncing. He could feel his ribs throbbing with his heartbeat. Acid burned in his throat until he couldn't hold it back anymore, and his stomach's contents splashed on the floor. It was all bile. He hadn't eaten in days, as the town was rationing during the siege. The town... Northpass... his home and family, all gone in an instant.

After a moment, things came into focus. Elvan allowed himself a breath, then glanced around. The room was metal with a wooden floor, and at one side of it came the rhythmic *fip fip fip* of an open tent flap in the breeze. In the distance, he could hear what he thought might be automated gunfire. It sounded like several weapons were firing at once, all to the beat of a metronome. Everything seemed severely out of place.

Elvan cradled his head with a groan as it throbbed with the flat *thump* of each weapon's report. The room continued to sway, and he felt like he might be sick again. But as he clenched his fists into the thin mattress beneath him and braced for boot-and-rally round two, he recognized the unmistakable calls of drivers to their steeds over the grind of heavy-duty wagon wheels on dirt.

Then it only took a brief instant to figure out he was in a caravan of sorts, moving at a steady pace along a semi-paved road. His stomach calmed, and his head stopped swimming. The distorted sounds coming from all around him sorted themselves out. What he thought was rapid artillery was actually the sound of horse hooves. He was in a wagon!

Only then did he notice a soldier in the other corner of the wagon. It was presumably the soldier who had captured him. He was asleep, and his face was now exposed. The man's uncanny battlemask sat in a basket on the shallow desk beside the large cot where he slept. He stirred and mumbled something, potentially roused by the stench of the boy's vomit. Even as the man's face twisted briefly in disgust, it seemed familiar. He might have been one of the Truydani defectors the people of Northpass took in. To Elvan, it didn't matter.

What did matter was making it out of there alive. So, Elvan decided to make a break for it while he still had the chance. He looked toward the back of the wagon, where a shaft of daylight shone in through the rustling tarp as it flapped in the low breeze. Just a few quick steps, a hop, and probably a roll off the road, and he would be free. He gathered up speed, took a breath, and made a break for the exit.

One step, two steps – he would find his siblings – *three steps* – he would find his mother – he pushed off hard on the fourth step, the skin of his foot scraping against the wood – he would break free and – *oh no.*

CLANNGGGG!

As he passed through the canvas curtain at the open end of the cart and lept toward the fading daylight, he smacked hard into metal bars. He heard a shout, then everything went black. It felt like a blink, but when he opened his eyes again, daylight had faded to the haunted gray of twilight. There was a leather strap holding his wrist to the wall beside the cot, and sitting at his feet was the soldier, deep annoyance evident on his face.

"Finally, you're up." The man's voice was coarse, like gravel in a metal chute.

Elvan moved to sit up, but pain surged through his body and head. He laid back down, but not before the breeze caught him and he shivered. The zing of fermented drink hit his nose, and he noticed his clothes were not dry. "Why am I wet...?"

"I dumped mead on you." The soldier waved a ram's horn mug in the air.

"... why?"

"To wake you up."

"Why?" Elvan touched a hand to his temple. Thinking *hurt*.

"Because we need to talk. Stop asking questions and maybe you'll make it out of here alive."

"Why should I trust you?"

"Don't trust anyone, kid. Just shut up and do what you're told."

Elvan had no reply to that. He could feel his stomach turn again. He must have looked as poorly as he felt, because his new companion shifted back and gave him a wary look.

"If you puke in here again, you're cleaning it up," the soldier warned.

Elvan clamped his mouth shut and shot a glare at his captor.

The man let his shoulders slack for a moment and sighed. "I'm sure you're a good kid. I saw what you did for your family, that was very brave. Very..." he hesitated a moment, finding the word, "stupid. While you were looking at me, there was another man behind you, ready to grab you and throw you in the brig with the others." He paused when he saw Elvan eye the metal bars at the back end of the covered wagon. "Trust me, this is a better situation than where he was going to put you. You're here because I saved you. We had orders to take the kids we found and send them to Kingsplot for training as frontline soldiers." He took a gulp from the mug.

"I don't understand why--"

"I'll stop you right there. Remember: *don't ask questions*. You're here with me now as my recruit, instead of in a camp where they teach you how to stand in front of the enemy as a human meat shield. Be thankful." He lifted the mug to drink again.

"Thanks, I guess," Elvan could feel himself slipping back into sleep.

The soldier splashed him with the drink once more. "Don't sleep; you hurt your head when you threw yourself against those bars. Did you really think that would work?"

"Don't ask questions," Elvan retorted.

The soldier smiled despite himself. "We'll get along

well. I'm Merven Stask. I'm a Truydani soldier, but I also go into battle looking for people who don't quite fit into the *human meat shield* mold. I think you will be a good fit for a new job we're developing."

Elvan stared at him bleakly.

"Come on, kid. You don't really have a choice in all this; just be happy I'm not giving you a death sentence."

Prayer

Scrubbers had the same routine every morning. Wake up, suit up, clean up. Where they were cleaning was always new, and where they retired at the end of their shift changed as often as the battlefront moved. There was always a team of scrubbers cleaning. Always. They worked around the clock in rotating shifts to keep the fungus at bay. For every ten soldiers, there was a team of twenty scrubbers, and for every company of scrubbers, there was a whole other company of scrubber support staff. The support staff were often soldiers who became too old or too injured to fight. They cooked meals for the scrubbers, moved camp as needed, and took care of one of the most important jobs a Truydani citizen could have: hygienics.

When scrubbers and soldiers returned from the battlefield, their gear was covered in the orange dust. It was not uncommon for them to have more than a few full-fledged flowering fungal attachments embedded in their armor or wrapped around their breathing tubes. The beast-plant thrived on decaying organic matter, which battlefields are chock full of. Hygienics specialists had the task of making sure none of it passed into the camp.

The process started with an herbicide bath. Scrubbers and soldiers walked slowly through the blue-lit corridor that hosed down every square inch of their gear. Then came the pressure wash, followed by another herbicide bath. After each cycle, they removed another layer of gear and clothing and were inspected by hygienics specialists. Rinse, and repeat. After the third round of this, they were assigned a steri-stall to disrobe. Their remaining clothing was carefully removed and stored in an air-tight container to be taken elsewhere for an even more thorough cleaning.

Fully nude, the team would then progress through another corridor for skin and hair cleansing via pressure-wash. Beet red and clean, they were provided a fresh set of "camp clothes" to wear. Even with this redundant and thorough system, there were occasional slip-ups where a spore or two would make it into camp and cause an infestation. But as souped-up as it was, the fungus was not unkillable. Only a few people would have to die if it was stopped early enough. So teams of hygiene specialists did sweeps all day and night across the camp, looking for fungus to kill and sections to quarantine.

But at the beginning of the scrubbers program, when the first wave of fun-guns were put into use, hygiene specialists did not exist, and any minor error was easily a death sentence to everyone in the camp. There was a learning curve, and Elvan witnessed it firsthand as a young man. The "new program" Merven Stask had taken him to for training was *really* new, and it ended up being just as deadly as the job he would have trained for at Kingsplot. The new super-weapon came with loads of setbacks that no one in the Truydani army was prepared to tackle. It was a messy, deadly time.

The Truydani scientist who developed the fungus into the super-powered weapon had anticipated it would be used as a long-range weapon, something they could fire from the ground into enemy territory. In theory, the fungus would land on the designated target, erupt out of the bomb-casing, and spread for a few days until there was no enemy or nest of Arachnids left to fight. Then, scrubbers would clean it up so Truydan could claim the land as theirs. The goal was to limit friendly casualties. Unfortunately, implementing his genius plan was not as simple as it seemed.

The same component that enabled the fungus to explode out of the bomb casing, which also allowed the fungus to take hold in previously inhospitable environments such as the desert, caused the fungus to become unstable at a certain altitude. Truydan's fungibombs frequently exploded prematurely, in mid-air, often close enough to the Truydani encampments that fatal infestations of entire companies were common when the bombs were used. Still, the fungus would often land close enough to infect the enemy territory -- but it spread so quickly and in such sporadic directions that scrubbers were rarely able to curtail the spread before the entire location went catastrophic. This led to the eventual use of close-range fungal weapons, called fun-guns, alongside traditional artillery, followed immediately by scrubbers and their canisters of fungicide.

By the time the latest wave of fungal weapons and protective gear were rolled out, Elvan had lost more comrades than he could count. He tried to remember them in his prayers at night, but he always forgot a name or two. Prayer was a tradition Elvan carried with him from Northpass, though he did not know who he was praying to. He'd known the name at some point, long ago, but it had been beaten out of him, the information booted from his brain to make room for more important things, like the proper method for approaching an orange bud as opposed to a deep red one. Like how to properly seal a mask and check an air hose for holes. Like how to unclog the valve for his canister.

Still, each time he left camp, each time he sprayed another bloom, he whispered a small prayer.

Lover

After three days' work and too many hours of decontamination protocol, scrubbers could enjoy a day of free time. They had to remain at the encampment in their authorized sections, but there were plenty of things to do in their own little tent city blocks that garnered much more enjoyment than wielding poison on the battlefield. As Elvan finally made his way to his tent in the hazy shimmer of sunrise, he stepped over the sprawled-out limbs of drunk scrubbers, heard the start of a scuffle as someone was caught cheating in a game of cards, and witnessed the mourning sounds of a musician's instrument coming into tune a few blocks south. On the low desert breeze, he could smell the beginnings of breakfast at the mess.

His tent looked exactly like all the others on his block, olive drab green with a black fringe. It sat a few feet away from the walkway to prevent mud from splashing into the living quarters. He poked his head in to find his bunk-mate, Ketil, sprawled out across the floor, one foot on his cot, the other tangled helplessly in the standard-issue scratchy wool blanket. His back end was exposed to the elements, and he was snoring. Evlan sauntered in, feeling the unstoppable grin tugging at his lips as he stooped and caressed that perfect pair of buns.

Ketil stirred. He let out an immediate groan of regret and clasped his head.

"Did I miss some kind of wild party last night? I must have passed half a dozen men out there in the same state as you." Elvan knelt beside Ketil.

"Did you cop a feel on all those other poor bastards, too?"

"No, K, I reserve that kind of harassment for you, and only you."

Ketil rose to meet his lips with a soft sigh. "Coffee?"

"Coffee."

"I promise we didn't get too rowdy," Ketil started, but as he said it, there was a clatter from the far corner of the tent, followed by an annoyed grumble.

"What's a man got to do to lie in a drunken stupor around here?" A groggy voice boomed from beneath a pile of cookware in the corner of their tent.

Ketil sighed and smiled at Elvan apologetically. "Okay, so maybe we got a little rowdy."

"Is that--?" Elvan began, swiveling to get a good look at the naked man dislodging himself from a particularly large stock pot.

"Devin? Yeah. He may or may not have stolen all the cook's gear from Bravo block."

Elvan stifled a laugh and did his best to look upset. It didn't work, and a sputtering giggle erupted out of him. "You... you did what now?"

Ketil threw his hands up. "Hey, don't look at me! It was all Devin!"

Devin groaned in the corner, then began his crawl for the exit, undoubtedly to go relieve himself.

"Devin, if you stick around, I'll make you coffee!" Elvan called after him. The only reply was the sound of inevitable retching after a night of partying a little too hard. "At least take your evidence with you, Dev!" Elvan called again.

There was a hiccup, an unintelligible attempt at a curse, and the sound of Devin's feet stumbling down the path toward his own tent.

Elvan and Ketil stared at each other with wide eyes and troublemaker grins.

"Would you believe he left his clothes here?" Elvan's sarcasm , as he wadded up the beer-stained clothes and threw them out the front flap. In a few moments, the smell of coffee filled the space.

"It's almost like he's still drunk or something," Ketil replied as Elvan sat beside him with two cups of the good stuff. He took his and nursed it. "Thank you."

"You owe me now," Elvan said, setting his cup down and leaning in for a kiss.

"Oh no, whatever will you ask of me?" Ketil chided just before their lips touched. Elvan climbed on top of him and pressed his broad brown body to his lover's. Ketil set the coffee down and reached for Elvan's face. "My love."

They had first discovered their mutual affection almost six months prior when Ketil moved into Elvan's tent after his former bunkmate was reassigned. Now, their frolicking was as frequent as possible. Every moment was treated like the potential last time they could be together. The life of a scrubber was a dangerous one. Death came quick, but it was never painless. Best to enjoy these pleasurable moments as the opportunities arise.

Ketil was known for making his way around camp, and Elvan liked that about him. He was fun, experienced, and skilled in the art of intimacy. And he chose to make his home with Elvan, to share a cot with him for more than just a good time. They often spoke of their lives before, their families lost, the things they remembered of the world outside the orange haze. They shared secrets and regrets.

Ketil had joined the ranks of scrubbers much later in life than Elvan, though their ages were roughly the same. He'd come from a wealthy settlement that had remained largely unharmed by the Arachnids before Truydan claimed it. He freely shared what knowledge he'd learned in his settlement with anyone who would listen. He taught many men in their unit how to read and write.

Unlike Elvan, Ketil was petite. His ever-growing, shiny brown hair was always swept back and secured in a single long braid – until he was off the clock. Then, once he shed the hazard suit and had a drink or two, his mane was loose, wild, and untamed. He was irresistible to Elvan, a forbidden fruit that must be tasted. And taste, he did.

Elvan took in Ketil's scent, hell-bent on burning the fragrance into his memory forever. There were teeth, and claws, and sighs, and edges in the lead-up, and then Elvan wound his fingers into the smaller man's hair, that perfect, seductive hair, and guided him into position.

"Tell me how much you want it."

"I need it, Elvan. Please..."

"Good boy."

It was a dance they knew well, but the steps were different every time, accounting for changes in rhythm, tempo, mood. They moved together like fire and air, pushing and pulling, breathing life into one another, sucking it back out. Thriving wildly until both were used up and spent.

Simply put: when they fucked, it was art.

But to Elvan, the true masterpiece always came after the main act. Ketil's face, the warm glow his body took on as he bathed in the post-coital atmosphere, the way his breathy voice ebbed and flowed with philosophy and poetry and mathematics? That was magic. Elvan liked to imagine that whatever god he prayed to was watching them in those moments, painting still-life captures of Ketil's beauty, writing plays to their cascading laughter and contented sighs.

Survivor

Elvan awoke to the rattle of tent poles. Ketil was still fast asleep in his arms. The dark living space came into focus as he blinked away the sleep, and the pounding in his chest came to the fore. Something was *terribly wrong*. Then, his nose caught it on the wind: the unmistakable stench of ochre spore ammunition.

"Get up!" He practically threw Ketil from the bed as he made a dash for the emergency mask-and-suit-kits.

"What's going on?" Ketil asked, catching the emergency pack Elvan tossed to him.

"The front shifted. The front shifted and they didn't tell us!" Elvan shouted above the not-so-distant boom of artillery. He scrambled to zip up the early-issue anti-spore suit, rushing to seal the rebreather on his face. He recalled the stories of battle taking a turn for the unpredictable and trampling any nearby scrubber camps in the way. He recalled hoping it would never happen to him.

"Wait... what?" Ketil had a leg in his suit, and his mask was on, but he wasn't moving fast enough. He must not have heard the stories. Or perhaps he was still a little drunk. Elvan did not have time to figure it out.

"Get dressed, K! We're exposed!" The sound of a spore rocket smacked the night as Ketil struggled with the suit's closure fasteners. There was a soft thump as the large grenade landed just outside their tent. "Get down!" Elvan tackled his lover to the ground, and the device exploded.

For a moment, there was pristine silence. Then, with a rush and a ragged breath, he was overwhelmed with the stimuli of a very active battlefield.

The dull ache in Elvan's head fed into the icy trill that dominated his soundscape. Anything beyond the ringing in his ears was muffled, like he was underwater. He tried to gather his bearings, shoving the tent's tangled and torn debris to the side, then rolling on his back to look at the carnage. Already, the orange dust was everywhere. Tendrils were quickly taking hold, but there was still time to escape.

He reached for Ketil, but his gloved hands grasped only debris. "Ketil! Where are you?" For a moment, there was nothing, then the pile beside him moved and his lover's face emerged. "Oh thank god..." He scrambled on his hands and knees to Ketil's side. "Come on, you have to get up, we have to go. We have to leave, *now*!"

Ketil just shook his head and his lips formed the word, "No." His eyes fluttered closed. He was pale, but it seemed like he had managed to get his suit and mask on in time.

Elvan figured he was probably concussed. He grabbed Ketil's shoulders and shook lightly. "You don't have time for a nap, love. We have to get off the battlefield."

Ketil looked at him groggily, tears pouring from his eyes. He tried to smile, but he gagged and coughed instead. Blood splattered the window of the rebreather.

Elvan's heart sank. He knew what it meant. He did not want to accept it. Ketil reached up and put his hand on Elvan's cheek. The airflow mask and glove kept their skin from touching. He felt it anyway. Elvan leaned in close, choking back tears. The ringing had subsided enough that he could hear his lover's voice with his ear pressed to the glass.

"Dying... Elvan. I... love... you..." Ketil forced the words out with the last air he had in his body, and his hand fell from Elvan's face as life left him.

When Elvan sat back up, trembling and broken, his love was a corpse. He pulled back the debris and searched Ketil for wounds. Along with many contusions and possible broken bones, he had been impaled through the back by the handle of the cook's ladle, straight into his chest from behind. The fungus had already taken root in the corpse through that hole and was feeding on the organs and still-warm blood inside. In an hour, there would be nothing left of Ketil for Elvan to mourn. Even now, there was no time. The *clink* of another spore rocket being loaded into a launcher forced him into action. He recited a prayer as he ran and searched for somewhere safe from the shelling.

As he ran, he managed to peel a working fun-gun off a corpse. In the distance, he could see the towering figures of Arachnids as the enemy rode them into battle. The unsettling hum of Coleoptera Arachnids, the dreaded battle drone bugs, vibrated his chest from somewhere above in the night sky. He fired off a few rounds at an enemy soldier sheltered behind a dead Arachnid. The man fell with a wavering scream as the fungus took hold. He was dead by the time he hit the ground. Elvan kicked the corpse out from the shelter of the dead bug and crouched, careful not to let the spindly wire hairs on the curled-in legs scrape a hole in his suit.

He scanned, looking for a way out of what appeared to be the center of the battlefield. Enemies were coming from the east, but the whole place was a mess of fighters charging and firing in all directions. Some soldiers fought hand-to-hand, while others followed after their foes with guns trained to kill. One very large Truydani man fired his fun-gun until it was out of ammo, then grabbed two of his enemies by their heads and smashed them together until they broke open like melons. He ran off after the rest of their squad with a chuckle, bounding like a big cat after its prey.

Suddenly, a host of gunfire whizzed past Elvan's face. He ducked back behind the megabug's thorax. It twitched when the bullets hit it, the legs lowering down over him like a dangerously hairy cage. As he crouched close to the ground, he spotted an automatic weapon peeking out from under the enemy he'd dispatched. He pried it out from under the body and took a deep breath. Without hesitation, he swung the weapon up, rested it on the thorax, aimed, and squeezed the trigger. With a sweeping motion, he shot the Arachnids out from under their masters, then swept back around to take out anyone who had survived the 12-foot fall. Then, he ran.

The nearest vehicles were a few blocks west. Elvan knew if he could manage to get inside one and get it going, he would have a bullet-resistant means of escape. He checked the oxygen levels in his emergency kit. He was almost down to 80%. Running would likely deplete it to 50% by the time he reached the vehicle. Still, he had to try. He fired at enemies, dodged grenades, and took out Arachnids with his gun as he went. By some miracle, the flimsy emergency kit suit was still completely intact when he finally got there. But he could feel time running out on his small fresh-air tank. It still had to last him the entire drive to the next encampment, which he would have to locate on the fly.

He jumped into the vehicle, cranked the starter, and hit the accelerator. With a reluctant hiss, the vehicle rolled forward. Shots bounced off the vehicle's shell with a *ting!* as he sped through the gates of the encampment and headed north.

Deserter

After almost eight hours of driving, he finally saw the gates of a Truydani encampment on the horizon. It was still nearly thirty minutes away, and the air in his tank had twenty minutes left, but his salvation hung near. He took to holding his breath, a technique they learned in training for survival in the event their air tank became compromised. Still, the rays of the afternoon sun were inescapable, and he felt he was being cooked alive. With each out-breath and gasp inward, he could feel himself becoming more and more dizzy. By the time he arrived at the gates, his vision was nearly gone, and he had moments left on his tank.

A gate guard approached the vehicle, and Elvan pointed to the tattoo under his eye that indicated his scrubber status and signaled for a decontamination team. Then, he pointed to his air tank, which was at 2%. He passed out right as the guard walked off to find a hygiene specialist and inform the proper authorities of their guest. Elvan awoke to the rush of fresh air as the mask was peeled from his face in a steri-stall. He couldn't control the trembling, the coughing, or the tears that followed. He blamed the oxygen deprivation, but the truth was he wept for the loss of his lover and his company. He assumed no one had made it out alive, or if anyone had, they were dead on the side of the road, deprived of air and unable to decontaminate well enough to remove their suit.

He was accompanied by security personnel through the pressure wash, then escorted, still nude, to the encampment's officer tent block. They paraded him up the road, feet now covered in mud, to the Chief's tent, where he was shoved inside and brought to sit in a chair in front of a very intimidating desk. There, he was provided a blanket and a cup of water while he waited for the company commander's arrival. He spoke for the first time since he arrived, addressing the guards.

"Which camp is this?" His voice came out hoarse. He sipped the water. It was warm.

"We're under orders not to tell you anything," one guard responded. He sounded apologetic.

"I understand," Elvan replied. He whispered a prayer. He'd been lucky enough to make it this far. He turned around to look at the guards. "But, it's not a scrubber camp, is it? This doesn't look like a scrubber camp."

"No, it's not." The voice came from behind him, from behind the desk.

Elvan whirled around and stared, wide-eyed. The man seated before him was Merven Stask. "...sir?"

"Hey kid." Merven sat and offered him a sip from his already-open flask. Elvan declined, gesturing to the warm water in his hand.

"I'm so glad it's you."

Merven paused and sighed before taking his seat. "I'm not."

"What do you mean?"

"... Kid... you're a deserter."

"I'm a what?" Elvan stood, feeling his cheeks flush to his ears. The guards shifted their weight, making ready to restrain him. Merven waved them out of the tent.

"You ran from a battle, El."

"I... I mean, I guess? I *survived*, Stask. There was no making it out of there alive. The front shifted in the middle of the night!"

"There was no making it out alive, yet somehow you show up at my doorstep in a vehicle and an emergency kit with enough oxygen to get here? It's suspicious. You're the only one who made it out–"

"That you know of!" The words lept out of Elvan. His vision swam.

"Right, that we know of. It doesn't look good. Are you telling me there are others, El?"

"No. I mean, I don't know. I didn't see anyone else." Stask wasn't wrong. I did look bad. He flashed back to Ketil, the wound in his back. "I did what I thought was right, I..." he sat back down, deflated, knowing excuses would do him no good. "What's going to happen to me?"

Stask looked at him knowingly and handed him the flask. Elvan took it willingly this time and took a shaky swallow of the hard stuff. Merven waited for him to hand it back before he spoke. "The punishment for desertion is death, kid."

Elvan sank lower, his head in his hands now. "But I'm not a soldier..."

"The wording in the manual makes it very clear. If you're in battle, you fight until you win, you die, or your commanding officer calls a formal retreat." There had not been a formal retreat since Truydan was founded.

"But this type of thing used to happen all the time... why did no one tell us we had to stay there until it was over?"

"It's in the manual."

"I didn't think--"

"I know you didn't."

There was a long pause. Elvan looked up at his old mentor, tears seeping out the corner of his eyes. Crying twice in one day. It was like he was a kid again, arriving at the scrubber training camp. "You said this," he made a sweeping gesture with his empty water cup, "wasn't a death sentence."

"Neither of us knew how hard that job would be. But this? It wasn't the job that killed you. No, this was all you."

Elvan's heart sank. "So how... how does it happen?"

"I do it. There's a hearing and some paperwork, and then a chopping block and... I do it."

"Fuck."

"Fuck is right."

They sat there in it for a moment, and then Elvan began to laugh.

Stask looked at him with wide, serious eyes. "It ain't funny, kid. You're dying tomorrow."

"He was impaled! By a soup ladle!" He leaned forward in his seat, shaking with manic laughter, tears threatening again like angry storm clouds in his eyes.

Merven looked at him, perplexed. "Do you hear me, kid? I have to kill you tomorrow."

Elvan looked up, suddenly sober. "The only reason I would want to stay alive, the only person who mattered is dead, Stask. I should have died with him last night. Coming here was... just postponing the inevitable, I guess."

Stask shook his head. "There are more things to live for than love, kid."

"Like what?"

Stask paused for a moment, eyes coming alight with realization. "... Revenge."

"Revenge?"

"Yes!" Stask stood and began pacing behind his desk, fervently stroking his chin. He turned to Elvan, something euphoric glinting in his eye. "You might not have to die tomorrow, El."

"What do you mean?"

"Remember how we met? How I would go to the sieges and recruit people for our new programs?"

"I mean, I wouldn't call it recruiting, but okay."

Stask waved away the snide remark. "There's a new program."

"But you're clearly not a 'recruiter' anymore."

"No, but I still have all my old connections – well, the ones who are still alive."

"... Stask, don't go pulling any strings for me. It didn't work so great the last time."

"You're still here, aren't you?"

"Well, sure but I don't know if I even want to--"

"Are you mad at the enemy for killing your boyfriend?"

"Of course I am. But I don't even know if it was them or us that did it."

"I'll pretend I didn't hear that last part, you treasonous bastard. Do you want to avenge his death?"

Elvan paused for a moment, thinking. Stask offered him the flask again and he took a drink, bracing himself against the sharp taste.

Stask knelt in front of him so they were eye to eye. It was much like how his father would talk to him after a long hard day. Merven always felt like a father to him, maybe more now than ever before. "El, I want you to live. You might not want to right now, but death is final. This will give you time to make that decision for yourself, instead of Truydan choosing for you."

Elvan met his eyes, took a deep breath, and committed. "Okay, let's do it."

Killer

The next morning, he was transported from Merven Stask's encampment straight to Kingsplot for retraining. En route to the training camp, he received a new tattoo under the scrubber label beneath his left eye. The new one branded him as a criminal. After completing his new training, which was a two-year process, he would receive yet another tattoo that indicated his new designation: supersoldier.

This training was unlike any he'd ever undergone. First, the recruits' bodies were punished to the point of breaking. After their true limits were identified, some were retired, and those who remained were brought in for surgery to receive cybernetic enhancements derived from Arachnotech. Many soldiers did not survive the transplants. It was bloody, gruesome business. Unlike their enemies, the ever-expanding city-state of Truydan did not condone the widespread use of Arachnotech or Arachnids as laborers. Anyone participating in the program agreed to lifetime servitude in their designated capacity, and to maintain this, Truydan's biggest secret. The only form of separation approved for those involved in the supersoldier program was death.

From there, the soldiers had to learn how to use their new bodies, weapons, and armor. Like the Arachnids, there were different subgroups of supersoldiers. Some were flamers, others were swordmasters, others wielded souped-up fun-guns, and so on. There was a supersoldier built and trained for every imaginable form of up-close combat on the battlefield. The common thread? Each one was equipped with a bioengineered resistance to the fungus, and all were given bodily enhancements that made them taller, broader, and more able to withstand the damage of a lifetime of battle. Elvan, who had been of medium build when he arrived at Kingslpot, often thought of his newfound height and breadth compared to the late Ketil, who had been quite small and spritely. As he trained, he focused on the word that had crossed Merven's lips as his sole reason to live: revenge.

His fellow supersoldiers all had their own reasons to fight. Some were born under the flag of Truydan, destined to carry it to victory on the battlefield. Others fought for honor and glory. Still, others fought for the thrill of it -- but none of that mattered to him. When he closed his eyes, all he could see was Ketil there, and then Ketil gone. Over the two years of learning how to run, push, and fight, his rage grew. He became something he never thought he'd be. His prayers were no longer humble requests for survival; they were dastardly utterances of vengeance to be exacted upon whoever and whatever lay in his path. They were curses.

Elvan was fueled by the fire of his anger. He let himself sink into it, used it to survive the hellscape that was his new life. Each night and each morning he would strive to remember his anger. Anger at his parents for not being strong enough. Anger at Merven Stask for taking and then abandoning him. Anger at Truydan for destroying everything and everyone he ever loved. Anger at the Arachnids for invading Earth in the first place. Anger at the fungus for tagging along for the ride. Anger at the world for making everything worse instead of trying to be better. And, finally, anger at himself for surviving all of it. And the day finally came he would have a chance to use that fire to exact his revenge on the world around him with the curse of his fun-gun and flame-pistol.

At last, he found himself toeing the line of the battlefield. Bulbous thunderheads rumbled in the distance like a herd of dark gray sheep stampeding toward him on tails of howling wind. He could see his foes advancing, settling into formations, checking their weapons. They had no idea what fresh hell he would rain down on them. His finger tickled the trigger of his gun, and he whispered another curse-tainted prayer. Beside him, battle brothers and sisters shifted on their feet, eager to spread their wings and get their first taste of real battle.

There was a command from a few rows back.

"Hold!"

The soldiers braced themselves.

The first shots were fired, cannon blasts exploded heaps of hot dirt and rock on the front line of supersoldiers that walled in the rest of the battalion. The fungus began to grow and spread from the pits the cannon balls created. Elvan stifled the urge to adjust the scrubber mask he no longer wore and had not worn for over a year now. Instead, he clenched the grip of his gun and took a deep breath. He was built to survive the fungus without so much as a sniffle or a sore throat. The smell was foul, sickly sweet, with a hint of decaying matter and fertilized dirt.

The next command followed the echo of more cannon fire.

"Advance!"

The supersoldiers moved forward, shoulder to shoulder, in lock-step formation with a perfect gait. They pressed on, explosions of dirt billowing out from all sides of them. Even when they were hit, the fodder only knocked them down. Winded, they would shake off the orange powder and get back up in time for the next command to advance further forward. Eventually, they halted, knelt, and put up their arm shields.

Small archers climbed into the crevices between their

hunched, hulking bodies. They took aim and fired on command, loosing all the arrows in their quivers. They were so small, some of them as young as he had been when Stask pulled him off that drainage pipe. Elvan looked across the line at the ruddy faces of the archers, and all he could see was an army of children, of innocents, captured from Northpass or any one of the other settlements Truydan had raided between then and now. His fury grew.

At last, the armies began a charge.

At last, he loped forward into the crowd of impossibly small humans, grown though they were, who dared challenge him to a fight.

At last, he would taste revenge.

He raised his gun and peppered the oncoming soldiers with a well-spaced seasoning of ocher. Blooms sprouted out of horrified faces. The screams echoed against the thunder. Flashes of gunfire mixed in with the lightning. The clouds hovered heavy and low now, as though night had descended on the field. To his left, a swordmaster cut down her enemies like trees, slicing them cleanly through the chest. A flamer expertly warded off an Arachnid to his right, causing it to rear up and toss its riders. It trampled nearby squads as it scurried off to safety.

The rain broke through the clouds in a deluge, slicking the ground and mixing the ichor, spores, mud, and powder into one vile mixture. Elvan barely recognized the sensation of bullets pelting his armor above the feel of the fat raindrops drenching them all from heaven. His boots gripped the turf beneath the wet mud as he charged toward the source of the gunfire -- it only took a few strides to meet that squad.

They turned tail and tried to run, but he was too quick. As he ran, he slung his gun back over his shoulder and reached out with both hands to grab the slowest of them. He raised the enemy over his head, and the world went silent as the wet *crackle!* of fragile human bones beneath his crushing, inhuman grip rippled from his palms, through his body, down to his feet. Elvan tossed the twitching, dying corpse aside and marched straight into the thick of the battle.

There, in the middle of the action, there was barely room to move. Bodies pressed against bodies, and arms swung, and weapons fired. Howls of bloody success and cries of agony sang out from all directions. It was a symphony of destruction. It was the soundtrack to his revenge. With each kill, he whispered another curse, another angry prayer, another vengeance mantra, christening it, making his work *holy*.

Every kill was a sacrifice to appease the dark, angry god he worshipped. If he did not know before that battle, he would certainly know it by the end -- that the god he prayed to, the god he cried out to, the god he begged to keep him alive and then begged to let him die alongside his lover, was only himself. As he fired, and snapped, and crushed, and swung, and punched, and blew fungus-filled holes into the faces of his country's enemies, he felt the anger in him begin to shift. In its place grew manic joy, righteous excitement, giddiness and spastic pleasure. That hungry pit in his soul was being filled for the first time in years.

By the time the battle ended, the field was flooded with water, blood, and ocher sprouts. The downpour had let up to a trickle, and the meditative calm and satisfaction that had filled him during those unrelenting hours of fighting began to fade. He could feel himself growing hungry again, even as he made his way back to camp for decontamination. He traced his finger along the tattoos beneath his eye and watched the sun come up over the scrubbers as they journeyed past him, making their way across the field to clean up his mess. He knew then that he was no longer a human. He was a god. He was a god of death and destruction, and he would never be rid of the bloodthirst that filled him.

6

COMPANION

MERLIN SPOKE & JB LETTERCAST

When aliens sleep... do they dream?

The smell of burning beans roused Jay from his musings. He lifted the can off the flame with a stick and nestled it in the rocks beside his perch. The hulking beast stirred quietly beside him, still clearly asleep. He wondered if he should wake it and offer it some food, but he didn't know if Arachnids even liked beans.

He hadn't seen his companion eat anything since they first crossed paths, which was a scary thought. How hungry did it have to be to decide to eat him in his sleep? To be fair, if it planned to eat him, it probably would have done so a long time ago. Jay's relationship with his unlikely companion was a curious one.

Jay wasn't an idealist. He knew that traveling with a vicious Arachnid as a companion was not likely to end well. Still, for the time being, it was practical. The thing could carry a lot of gear, and its presence seemed to ward off other Arachnids and bandits alike. Why it had chosen to tag along with him specifically, Jay had no clue.

He didn't understand a lot of things the alien did. And how could he? It wasn't like he could just ask his companion why it chose to save his life just a couple weeks ago. And even if he could ask, he wasn't sure he wanted to look that gift horse in the mouth. For all Jay knew, the alien was waiting for him to lead it to a populous village where it could have a smorgasbord of human-flavored treats.

But speculating was not going to do Jay any good. The spider had pulled its weight so far, helping him transport and sell salvaged wares as they traveled the main trade route without asking for a single thing in return.

Does he feel like I owe him? He caught himself. *No, not him. It. It's a monster, not a pet.* Jay felt guilt for thinking it, but he chalked the errant feeling up to his having given the damn thing a name. Even still, he wanted to reach out and pet the beast in apology.

He furrowed his brow at the slumbering monster and slurped some beans into his mouth from the still-hot can, thinking back on how their journey together began.

The Battle at Massdock

Rumors of invasions at nearby settlements had become increasingly common in recent months. Jay had seen the wreckage on some of his longer trade routes, but he never imagined the aliens would come for their little town of Massdock. But then, no one ever imagined the impending destruction of their beloved home. It's always someone else's home, somewhere far away. Until it's not.

Thankfully, Truydan was prepared. They had sent troops to help defend Massdock and the other vassal states in the area, then recruited all able-bodied citizens into a small militia. Jay and his people had had some time to prepare. They expected to fare better than the surrounding settlements that had refused to join Truydan's growing amalgamation of tributary and vassal states. But the civilian army was far from truly prepared for what was to come.

The alien onslaught was the stuff of nightmares. It was full-on war, army against army. Truydan's soldiers sent volley after volley of firepower at the approaching beasts, but the enemy did not slow in its approach. After two days of this, both sides finally arrayed against each other in full force.

Soldiers poured out from behind the wall like a swarm of hornets, and the front lines crashed into a terrible melee. Towering supersoldiers wrestled the creatures to the ground, blowing holes in thoraces, hacking off mandibles and arachnotech with Damascus swords the size of an average man. The plan was that Truydan's mutated soldiers would thin the ranks enough to make it so the humans could follow behind and help finish off the weaker beasts.

Jay and his trainband watched as the invaders' blood stained the ground a deep, blackish-violet. The supersoldiers were magnificent, hulking fighters, built to take a punch or ten, but they were not gods. Before long, the reddish-brown of human-type viscera began to mix in with the purple-tinted muck.

"Move out!"

The command caught Jay by surprise. It seemed too soon for his unit to be called to the battlefield. His heart raced as he donned his helmet and adjusted his armor for the last time. They marched down from their palisade perch and watched the unit before them deploy out into the trenches they'd dug in the weeks prior.

Then it was their turn. Jay's heart beat hard as they sprinted from one small patch of cover to the next. Different groups were sent to different parts of the field as they passed from one checkpoint to another. At one point, a huge swatch of acidweb took out the tail end of their trainband. The supersoldier who led them barely seemed to care.

Amidst the chaos, Jay tried to understand what their plan might be. But that seemed to change as the conditions on the battlefield developed. He saw the supersoldier give orders to the squad leaders from time to time, but the only thing he could hear above the roar of battle was his own thudding pulse. At his best guess, their trainband was being sent out to different spots on the battlefield to bottleneck the beasts.

Eventually, Jay's squad and one accompanying squad were the only troops following the supersoldier who had led them out of the settlement. They were on the far south end of the battle, facing the settlement wall. They watched as supersoldiers tried to forge a path toward their position near the rear of the Arachnid complement. Occasional bursts of fire came from the trench across from them, just to the southeast, which had the effect of either distracting or wounding the Arachnids that packed the field between the two ditches.

Jay crouched in the mud, his back pressed hard into the shelf of the trench. As ordered by their leader, both squads were hunkered down, waiting for their next turn to distract the bugs. His hands tingled, and his skull vibrated with every booming explosion. His lean muscles pulled taught in preparation to spring up and shoot, then drop back down before the enemy could melt his face off.

After a few rounds of fire-and-duck, something possessed Jay to get up and look over the wall of their pit. He glanced over to see if their leader was looking – he wasn't – then inched his way up to the top of the ledge, weapon pointed toward the enemy, finger on the trigger. He wasn't going to shoot; he just wanted to look. He peered into the scope, watching the grass wave faintly in the breeze of the oncoming nor'easter.

He caught glimpses of squads closing in on the aliens from behind as the supersoldiers attacked from the front. He watched as the troops in the trench across from him made a break for it. They dashed up the wall of their ditch and into position beside some of the other squads. Meters ahead of the squad, a supersoldier stabbed his sword up into the thorax of a towering beast. A shower of purple dowsed him, splashing the ground and turning the soil a sickly violet.

The other squad moved closer as the alien crumpled and flipped upside down in defeat, its dying wail attracting the attention of Arachnid-reinforcements. The militia squad charged, weapons drawn. Some yelled as they ran; others grimaced. A few trailed behind, either wounded or hesitant. Those were the ones who died first, picked off by a beast hiding in the very trench the squad had come from.

As he watched the carnage unfold through his scope, Jay felt a heavy, metal hand grab his shoulder. He jumped, accidentally squeezing the trigger. He didn't have a chance to see where the errant blast went because as soon as the shot fired, he was thrown hard to the ground by their metal-clad leader. He lay, dazed, at the supersoldier's feet for a moment before scrambling to stand.

"We're next!" He heard the supersoldier's muffled voice for the first time ever. It was just barely loud enough to distract from the cries of his doomed neighbors from across the field. The unsentimental voice came out warped and fuzzy through the amplifier mounted over the mouthpiece of his helmet. "Be ready!" With that, he turned on his heels, scanned the group once more, and gave the command. "Double time, move out!"

The Invaders

Squad leaders repeated the command, and the troops climbed out of the crumbling trench. They slinked quietly through the tall grass and smoke in the direction of a particular cluster of the hairy bastards. Jay struggled not to glance over at the half-eaten bodies of their neighboring squad. A nearby explosion left him coated with the pungent mixture of soil and vitals and threw his squad to their bellies for cover. They crawled further onward, following single-file until they were in position.

Battlesign from his squad leader indicated a hold for 30 seconds, followed by a charge to the northeast. From there, he assumed they were each on their own. They were really about to be left to their own devices to battle twelve-foot demons that could bring down a supersoldier with the angry sweep of a thorax or the thoughtless downward thrust of a boneblade-tipped appendage. And all his people had to fight back were guns they barely knew how to aim.

He clutched his weapon, counting to thirty. But his squad would never make the charge. Just as he reached ten seconds in his countdown, a bomb tore its way through the group's center from behind. Jay tumbled across the ground, blind, deaf, disoriented. He skidded to a halt with a squelchy thud, sprawled out in a spread-eagle hug of mother earth.

Jay's head spun as his vision and hearing restored themselves. He woke up, his back to the settlement. The explosion had flipped him over so that his head was pointing in the direction the bomb came from when he came to. His was vision filled with the silhouetted figures of more Arachnids approaching against the graying sky. They stalked toward him as if in slow motion, like eerie skyscrapers, all joints and legs. Walking alongside them, and in far greater numbers, were ghastly, gangly, unfortunate shapes. They seemed oddly human-like and altogether impossible in form.

He blinked hard, trying to understand the ghastly nightmare unfolding before him. All the while, the world struggled to right itself amidst his concussion. These bipedal creatures – no, only some of them were bipedal – seemed to be working with the alien forces to attack his people. They wielded weapons he'd never seen before, even on his long journeys across the trade routes that took him to the fringes of society.

His stomach turned as the blurry shadows refined themselves into detailed images. These things might have been human at one time, but no sane man would call them human now. They were even more mutated than the supersoldiers. Their skin was stretched in odd directions, with machines, weapons, tools, all embedded into their bodies in uncanny configurations. One of their kind towered above the rest on tall, sharp spires made of bone, its height matching that of the Arachnids. Another sported six eyes that took up its entire face.

Was that... arachnotech?

Before he could take in any more details, he felt a metal hand clasp hard at his back. He looked over his shoulder, neck screaming in pain as he craned to look at the supersoldier. Jay felt his eyes water, though whether it was from pain or emotion, he couldn't tell.

"You're alive," the supersoldier said as if reassuring Jay that this was neither a dream nor had he yet earned his passage into the afterlife. The horror was absolute, and they needed to get moving. "Follow me."

Jay found himself being tugged forward by the scruff of his armor before he could figure out how to move his arms and legs to crawl toward the nearest trench. Finally, he found his voice around the same time he remembered how to move with a purpose. "How many did we lose?"

"You don't need to know that," the Truydani soldier replied. "Keep crawling."

They made it back to the edge of the trench unnoticed and tumbled in. The supersoldier was clearly weakened, either depleted from battle or wounded from the blast, but Jay decided not to bring it up. Instead, he chose to assess his own physical state as the Truydani man set about contacting anyone who could help reinforce their position against the surprise attack that took out most of the remaining militia.

During his assessment, Jay realized he'd lost his helmet. His weapon was missing, too. He glanced anxiously around the trench in the dimming light, searching for replacements. Another explosion rattled his teeth and shook the dirt loose around him. It exposed a gun and the hand of someone he probably knew. With a silent apology, he pried the weapon from the stiffening pale fingers and positioned himself beside the supersoldier, who had clearly had no luck reaching anyone else.

"My radio must be down," the soldier said, annoyed.

"Is it just us?" Jay asked, fear tainting his voice. He didn't feel afraid, but his voice caught like he was about to cry.

"Looks like it." The soldier limped toward him, then leaned onto the embankment almost casually.

"Should we try to take out those... *things*?" Jay gestured with his gun to the field above them.

The hulking soldier gave an incredulous chuckle. "You don't stand a chance against them."

Jay swallowed dryly, tasting sweat, iron, and dirt. "What are they?"

"They're bad. That's all you need to know," his metal-clad companion said before shimmying up to the ledge. "And they've almost passed us. We might be able to run to join the other forces in retreat through the southeast trench line. What's your name, kid?"

"Jay. And I'm not a kid."

"Okay, Jay. I'm Evander. From this point on, we're battle buddies. We watch each other's backs until we're to safety. You don't go anywhere without me. Do *not* leave my side unless I tell you to. Got it?"

Jay nodded, his voice vanishing at the thought of running out onto the battlefield again. His knees shook, and his head throbbed, and he wondered if they were even winning the battle. He doubted it. And then it donned on him how much it didn't matter to him if they won because he probably wouldn't be around to help rebuild the town anyway.

I'm going to die today, he thought. Somehow the concept of battle hadn't been real until that very moment, in the trench, as he and a Truydani supersoldier named Evander waited for the alien enemy and their grossly altered human-like pets to pass.

"Okay, on my mark," Evander said from his perch at the trench ridge.

Jay nodded, though Evander wasn't looking.

"Alright," Evander breathed, "Now!"

And just like that, they were moving. Jay had never run

so hard or fast in his life. He was met with the noise of gunfire and the whipping sound of bullets flying past as he followed Evander in the direction of the trench across the field, which was still a world away.

Someone was yelling, and Jay only realized the battlecry was coming from himself when a laser blast sent Evander flying, and the world suddenly went quiet. His throat felt raw, and he couldn't breathe, but he kept going. Now it was only Jay, a merchant who hadn't seen any battle before today, running for his life through the pink mist that had once been his only hope of surviving this whole ordeal.

Without looking, he fired some shots to the east. He could hear the buzz of a laser cannon charging up to fire. Another fusillade peppered the space around him, and something fast and leggy approached in his periphery. This was it, this was the end, and he knew it. He stopped, still meters away from the trench, turned, and aimed.

If I'm going down, I'm going down fighting.

He braced himself for a painful death, firing all his shots without thinking to conserve any ammunition for the future. He imagined what it must feel like to be ripped apart by bullets or blown to oblivion by cannon fire. He imagined it so well that he could feel himself disintegrating as he shot arbitrarily at the enemy.

He should have died. He almost wanted it. Oblivion must be better than this. And he would have found his place among the beetles and worms if not for the hairy blur that came dashing toward him, deflecting the bullets that would have made his grave. The Arachnid absorbed most of the fire without a second thought. He watched its dripping mandibles descending toward him, intent upon devouring this tasty morsel before it expired. He braced for the burn of acid and the sting of fangs.

And then something happened.

The spider missed, jaws passing over him until it towered above him like a mother fox protecting its babies. It whirled toward the gunshots and screeched. There was a sudden spray of violet blood from its face right before it collapsed. The total weight of it hit Jay, knocking the wind from his chest, and for some time, he just left his body.

Jay lay there, crushed by the hairy, smelly, lukewarm weight of that alien beast. They were in the middle of a battlefield, surrounded by enemies. Neither of them was meant to survive this encounter. Somehow, that truth came to him as he waited to slip into the end of all things.

The Octoped Savior

He swam around the dark for a while, mind wandering to memories he hadn't conjured up in ages. Childhood. The taste of ale and sweet buns after a long day of working the field with his father. The acrid smell of dust and spores on the wagon trail at the fringe of the Orange Frontier. The vibrant green of rolling clover fields in late spring as he made his way homeward for the trade fair.

He had no idea how long he had lain on death's doorstep. When he came to, his savior was nestled behind him, a large piece of shrapnel lodged in its face. It twitched from time to time but seemed more helpless than hostile. His entire body ached. Smoke filled the sky. His town had been destroyed like all the others. The Truydani soldiers had left, or maybe all died. No one had come to clear the bloating corpses strewn across the field. Enemy forces were nowhere to be seen.

No Arachnids. No mutants. No civilians. Just the stench of decay and the crackle of fires burning themselves out behind the city walls. The stillness was uncanny after the chaos of battle. Weaponless, with half his armor torn off him, Jay felt exposed. But his gun had been crushed by the weight of the beast that now cowered like a nervous dog beside him. If the gun still worked, he would shoot the cursed thing. Not out of pity but for vengeance.

Smoke and tears stung his eyes as he wandered the field, looking for anything he could use. The spider followed him, hunkered low, nursing its wounds. He wept as he searched the disfigured corpses of people he knew, hoping to find a weapon that wasn't out of ammo or charge. A few hours later, he reached the gate, having only found a broken switchblade knife and some stolen rations.

He stepped through the gaping hole in the palisade wall, tiptoeing around hardening gobs of acidweb and side-stepping over heaps and piles of bodies from both sides, all the while followed by the beast that had saved his life. Eventually, he reached the center of town, one of the many places where he used to sell his wares.

The fountain at the center of it, built when he was only a few years old, lay in a heap of rubble. He knelt at its base, wishing he had listened to the tales the elders told of life before the settlements. He thought he'd always have everything he needed, even on the road when things were scarce. But his home was gone, along with everything else he had stored up for emergencies. He had nothing to trade and no one to trade it with.

The beast nudged him with a sticky pedipalp, and rage suddenly bit through the grief and fear. He whirled on the thing and threw a chunk of the broken fountain at its face. The spider flinched when the debris made contact but didn't leave. Instead, it just looked at him with the eyes it had left, blinking occasionally.

"What do you *want* from me?!" His voice bounced off the busted walls. "You want to eat me? Huh? Here, take a bite!" He thrust his forearm at the imposing, hairy thing, which just continued to stare at him, head tilted. A spark of electricity danced along the machine mounted to the top of its head, and its whole body twitched. Jay felt a twinge of -- guilt? Perhaps it was pity? -- when he noticed the slow leak of blood and other fluids dripping from where the shrapnel was embedded in the Arachnid's face.

He remembered a wounded dog that came to their city gates when he was younger. Half the town wanted to kill it, to keep it off the cattle. The other half of the town, his mother included, wanted to help it. They ended up fixing its leg, and it seemed to understand that it owed them its life. It never left the city gates and died years later, fending off a pack of wild dogs that had managed to get into a chicken pen.

Jay could hear his mother's voice in his head.

"The poor thing is injured. It's just looking for help."

He looked at the spider, which gave another full-body spasm. Slowly, he reached his hand out again. It didn't do anything, just stared like it had been since he woke up.

"Why did you save me?" He asked it, voice trembling with exhaustion and sadness. Of course, the spider would never answer that question, no matter how many times he asked it on their journey southwest. So, then and there, at the gravesite of his old life, Jay decided to return the favor. Still shaking, he petted the coarse hairs on one of its pedipalps. "I guess it's just us, now..." he rested his hand on the beast, and for the first time since he learned the Arachnids were headed to his hometown, his heartbeat began to slow. "Alright," he said, with a sigh, "let's get out of here."

The Westward Road

The road out of Massdock had never been a busy one, but it was eerily empty in the wake of devastation that had razed the nearby vassal states. They passed by ghost town after ghost town, stopping each time to search for survivors, supplies, and anything they could use for trade. Some of the places still had a few people left in them. Any goods Jay managed to salvage or trade were as damaged as the people he got them from.

No one they came across took too kindly to his companion. Some villagers even chased them away from their town gates. Eventually, they managed to get a cart for wares, some makeshift saddlebags for the spider, and enough food to last the one-way trip to the edge of the Orange Frontier, where Jay's favorite artificer lived. Jay assumed the spider would want hot food. *Live* food. There would be plenty of small game this time of year along that road.

The trek was easier than Jay remembered, even as he recovered from the beating he took at the battle at Massdock. In the past, he'd always made his way westward against the ticking clock of winter frost. But now, in the dying hour of springtime, he and his companion were greeted by fair weather. The mornings were soft and warm, and just as the afternoon reached its peak heat, they were cooled by gentle drizzles that melted away to reveal a magnificent sunset.

At first, Jay tried catching rabbits for his companion. He brought the stripped and cleaned carcasses to the camp and presented them to the spider, but it only stared at him in that half-cocked way it always did. So he cooked up the rabbit and stowed it for the next day, then set a snare that would catch the rabbit and keep it alive.

When he checked the trap the next morning, he was pleased to find a larger hare, panting and exhausted from fighting against the snare. He led the spider to the creature, but again, the thing just looked at him. So he let the hare go since their bags were full of rabbit meat from the night before, and they moved on.

At one point, about halfway through their trip to see the artificer, they came across a group of other people. Jay had known about them for a couple days. The smoke from their evening campfire had never moved, and Jay wondered if they had set up a trading post during his time away from the trail. But as he and the spider neared the spot where the fire should be, there was no trading post to be seen.

The sun was still up but setting quickly. In the dimming light, he could see a dark fire pit filled with more than a week's worth of ashes and the signs of a camp that picked up and moved swiftly. There was no indication of a struggle, no bodies, no spiders, no orange spores.

"I wonder if they saw us coming and decided to move camp." Jay had taken to speaking to the spider regularly by this point. He never expected it to respond, and it never did. They nestled into a small grove of trees to the side of the fire pit, where Jay could keep an eye out in case the people returned. He propped up against one of the trees, belly full of squirrel, and dozed off.

He'd been asleep for some unknowable amount of time when he awoke to the sound of an old-world gun being cocked. It took him a moment to register the cool of the barrel pressing to his temple. In the light of the full moon, he could see the silver silhouettes of about seven people surrounding their camp. The spider was nowhere to be seen. His vision pounded with his heartbeat, but he tried not to show his fear.

Slowly, he raised his hands. "I'm sure we can work this out–" a fist came down and rattled his jaw. His vision swam, and he spat blood onto the grass.

"We'll be taking your stuff now." He couldn't tell where the voice came from.

"Go ahead guys; I think it's just him," the person with the gun said, gesturing over to the cart to Jay's right.

"Why are you doing this?" Jay asked.

"Does it matter?" The gunman asked.

For a moment, the only sound was the noise of rummaging through the goods on the cart. Then, Jay spoke again. "I'm Jay."

"I don't care," the fingers flexed their grip on the gun. It wasn't hesitation; it was a threat.

"Please, I lost everything... this is all I have."

"I guess you didn't lose everything then, did you?"

A scream came from a few yards behind the tree where Jay sat, and the gunman pointed his weapon toward it. There was a second wail, then a crunch.

"What the fuck?"

There wasn't time for anyone to answer the question because suddenly, another person was snatched up into the canopy.

"No, no, please!"

CRUNCH!

Blood spilled through the leaves like thick rain on a summer night. In the span of a breath, bullets flew. One ricocheted off something and caught one of the robbers in the face. Someone else was pulled into the canopy. Acidweb shot out and melted the skin off another. The gunman still hadn't moved from his position, but Jay seized the confused moment and disarmed the thief.

After a few moments of carnage, it was only the two of them among the *drip drip drip* of viscera from the treetop. Jay had the gun to the person's head. They looked up at him in terror, blood streaks like black against the dusty silver of their skin in the moonlight. The spider had done its part, and now it was time for Jay to do his. He squeezed the trigger, and brain matter sprayed the ground where their embers lay dying in the fire pit.

In the east, the sun was beginning its ascent. The spider crawled down from the tops of the trees, covered in blood. As the light improved, Jay could see that it wasn't injured beyond what had happened to it at Massdock. He gathered up what the thieves had dropped around the camp, then set to clearing the bodies of anything else that might be of use.

By the time the sun poked its head above the eastern mountain range, they were back on the road.

"Thanks. Again," Jay said.

The Artificer's Homestead

Still haunted by the encounter with the thieves, Jay struggled to sleep. The monster had no fear. Sometimes it even snored as it napped. He leaned against it, grateful to have the thing nearby in case of any other unexpected visitors. Tomorrow, they'd enter the township of Garreth, which is really just a string of very distantly placed homesteads along the outer ridge of the Orange Frontier.

The artificer, Everist, would not be expecting them. This was not the time of year she and Jay would usually see each other, and she certainly would not expect him to have a spider as a traveling companion. But he knew she'd understand why he chose to see her for this particular task.

Everist lived on the fringes of society with good reason. Her ideas about the space invaders were far from conventional, and her genius-level understanding of their tech earned her all kinds of uncomfortable looks from most of the civilized folk.

Jay had slept a few hours before the sunrise roused him. He kicked dirt over the fire, and he and his alien companion made their way toward Garreth. It was a short walk compared to the rest of the journey. Two small hills, about four miles from that night's camp, framed by the Orange Frontier. It stretched out, an insurmountable wall along the southwestern horizon.

They reached Everist's homestead by lunchtime. At the front gate was a rare piece of technology, a communication system that allowed Everist to talk to whoever was at her gate. Jay pressed the button, which made a buzzing sound on both ends of the intercom. After a moment, the speaker crackled to life.

"No visitors."

"Ev, it's me."

"Me who?" He could hear the clatter of something in the background.

"Jay. It's Jay."

"Jay...?"

"Massdock. The merchant." There was a pause, and Jay was about to press the button again, but the front gate swung open with a sharp squeal.

"You have a spider on your back," Everist said when she met them on her front porch.

"Yeah, I came to ask for a favor for him, actually."

"How do you know it's a him?" Everist asked, circling the creature, which gave out an electrified shudder.

"I don't."

She reached out and petted the Arachnid, eying the shrapnel in its face. "What happened?"

"Massdock is gone." It physically hurt him to say it.

"I thought it was a rumor," she said, glancing back at him. Her eyes glinted curiously, and she brushed a hand over the shaved side of her head.

"I'm only here because of him," Jay said, gesturing to the alien.

"Weird. Did you train him?"

"No. It – *he* – saved me and just sort of followed me around after that."

"Most peculiar..."

"Twice, actually. So I figure I owe him."

"You want me to remove this?" Her fingers grazed the curved edge of the shrapnel.

"If you can. It seems to be hurting him. He gets these... I don't know what to call them. Seizures? Tremors?"

"I think I can do that, and I have parts that can fix the tech on its head, too."

"What'll it cost?"

"Nothing. He's a tame spider. If we fix this, there's hope we might be able to learn how to communicate with them. We might be able to fix this whole mess yet!"

Jay knew it would be useless to tell her that any efforts to "fix" the world would end in bitter disappointment, so he kept his mouth shut and watched as she led the creature inside and mixed a special concoction to help it sleep through the surgery. He did not ask how she knew so much about bugs and their tech. He did not want to know. Even if he *had* wanted to know, he felt that no matter how well she tried to explain it, he would never really understand what she meant. Mad scientists always talk in complex languages and secret codes.

He slept for most of the surgery, finally able to sleep soundly in the shelter of a real house after too long without a home. The fitful dreams that had plagued him since the battle let him have his rest, and for the first time since being crushed beneath the spider, pleasant, empty darkness was his only companion.

He awoke to a dark room, the last rays of the dying sun coloring the horizon. At the back of the house, Everist labored beneath a bright white light. She had removed the shrapnel and was finalizing her repairs on the tech in the creature's face.

"I thought you left," she said, wiping sweat from her forehead with her sleeve.

"Thanks for letting me rest here."

"I think you should stay awhile," she said. "Hand me that over there," she pointed to some instrument Jay had never seen before. He grabbed it and handed it to her.

"Why?"

"You have nowhere to go, and this thing might miss you when you're gone." Jay was about to decline when he saw the spider's leg twitch. Everist paused and glanced up at him. "Don't worry, it does that sometimes," she returned to her work with a tight smile, "besides, it's safe here."

Jay sat, sinking deep into an ancient and fluffy chair in the corner of the room. "I suppose I could–" the spider twitched again. "Are you sure that's safe?"

"Oh yeah, it's totally–"

But before Everist could finish her sentence or her work on the arachnotech, the spider jumped up and swept its pedipalps across the room. It stood at its full height for the first time since the battle at Massdock and gave out a menacing bellow.

"Run!" Jay yelled, pushing a confused Everist out of the room.

They weren't fast enough. Everist tripped over a pile of scrap-tech, and the spider caught her in its maw, clamping down with a slicing and bitter crunch. Blood sprayed all over the ceilings, the walls, the furniture, and Jay, who cowered in pure terror.

"Please don't do this... I thought..." but Jay caught himself. What had he thought? That they were friends? That this malevolent monster had saved him out of the kindness of its heart? That he could reason with the aliens that had been hunting and eating his kind for decades now? He turned and ran for the door. He would be damned if he died of his own incompetence. He dashed past piles of random junk, knocking stuff over to slow down his pursuer.

Artificers' places always have the strangest collection of items, he thought to himself as he scanned the scene for anything he could use. He yanked the door open and rattled the doorjamb just enough that something like a harpoon fell from its mount above the entryway. It hit him hard, but he managed to catch it, swinging it by the strap over his shoulder just in time to jump out of the house and slam the door on the monster's gaping jaw.

The Fate of Merchants and Monsters

The night air was humid and hot, fireflies glowed in the tall grass, and the silence of the plains seemed eerie in contrast to the carnage he'd just narrowly escaped. No, was still trying to escape. He could go for the front gate! Or he could try to find a hiding spot somewhere along Everist's homestead property line and hope the beast would head in the direction of the noisier villages to the south.

Or he could try to kill it. His heart hurt to think about things ending like that. He'd lost everything, but that beast had given him his life when he should have been dead twice over. Did he dare meet death for a third round, with the alien as the referee? He wouldn't have a chance to make that choice.

Silently, from the treeline behind him, a herd of Arachnids and gaunt humanoid figures crept through the grass. A twig broke, and he turned just in time to see the hungry hoard descending upon him. As he lay dying in the grass, he saw the blurry visage of his companion as it burst out through the wall of the homestead and joined its comrades. The last thing he saw was the dark chasm of its gaping mouth against the night sky. The last thing he felt was its chelicerae clamping tightly around his skull. The last thing he heard was his own screams as he spiraled out into the darkness of death.

7

VERIDIAN FALL

JB LETTERCAST

"I NEVER WANTED it to come to this. None of us did." The Priest's woeful voice carried through the underground cathedral, seeming to come from all directions. Normally, the gray-brown walls of earth would muffle any noise inside the hive, but not here. The shape and arc of the room perfectly amplified the voice of the speaker, while countering the murmurs and whispers of any wayward parishioners.

Purple-domed windows along the ceiling let in just enough elegant, ghostly light to illuminate the speaker, who, in this case, was Master Priest Eloqueth Charter, himself. His surgically mutated face glowered over the edge of the pulpit. Gaunt shadows stark under his jowls against the purple that tinted what was left of his pale skin. The congregation looked like ants from his place on the platform at the head of a large cavernous room in the converted Arachnid nest.

Charter was an elderly man, though it was hard to tell who was old and who was young beneath layers of cybernetic augmentations. His bony frame poked sharply against the baggy, indigo robes that indicated his sacred position in the nest-city. From his sleeves protruded long, spindly appendages, harvested from the bone spires of deceased cavalry-class Arachnids. The white bone was thinly wrapped with muscle tissue, wiry ligaments, patchy red skin, and thick tubes, all leading from the mechanipack installed at his shoulders, down to his robotic fingers.

The arms were long enough to carry him through the nest like a pair of legs, elevating him above the masses. He was too holy to walk on the ground like the commoners. These grotesque additions would have been his most distinguishing feature were it not for the All-Seeing Eyes, ever-rotating and focusing like kaleidoscopes, dominating the landscape of his face. The eyes were the most haunting aspect of any Master Priest. The ghoulish contraptions could quite literally see into the soul, or so the parishioners were told. There was some truth to that. The augmentations allowed the user to see in a wide range of wavelengths, including a type of special vizion the cyber-acolytes had come to call Shadow Sight.

Only truly worthy Tyropriests were elevated to the status of Master Priest, and the test of their worthiness was dangerously effective. The Tyropriest would undergo the surgery, losing their human oculi and much of their facial structure to make way for the All-Seeing Eyes. Then, as they recovered over the next few months, the Tyropriest would begin learning how to see again. If their mind could handle the new tool without breaking, they were deemed worthy of being a True Priest. If they could correctly interpret the Shadow Sight, they were elevated to the status of Master Priest. Most Tyropriests never regained their vision. Those were renamed as Downpriests. As a mark of their station, they wore a black shroud over their heads. The shrouds served a second purpose – they hid the gruesome contortions of the Downpriests' broken face as they served the conclave from the shadows.

Charter could see a small gathering of Downpriests in the back of the congregation now. Some had been his fellow Tyropriests in the times before his transformation. Without an ounce of bitterness, they had become his secret allies as he rose to the top of their order. They were his little birds among the flock, listening and reporting on the private goings-on of the lives of those in the conclave and their parishioners.

It was those same Downpriests standing at the back of the room who had helped him uncover the insurgence festering in their burgeoning hive. And now, it was time to purge the traitors. All throughout the nest, Dutymen stood in doorways, behind workstations, in the feasting hall, in the surgical center, ready for him to give the order. He shifted and clicked the collar-radio on his throat to broadcast on all channels. When he spoke again, he could hear his voice echoing from the myriad corridors around the cathedral.

"But there are those among us who have plotted against our peaceful mission. They cannot be trusted." That was the cue. From the fringes of the congregation came twenty-or-so Dutymen, who walked between the pews of bowed parishioners. "Bring them to me." Gasps and cries echoed through the place as the large Dutymen pulled select parishioners from their prostrate positions and dragged them by any means necessary to the front of the room.

All around the nest, people were pulled from their duty stations, their beds, the latrine, the food hall, and brought to cower at the foot of the pulpit. The ordeal took almost two hours, all the while, the rest of the citizens who were loyal to the hive filed into the cathedral and bowed in respect to the

Master Priest. At last, all one hundred and eighty-four citizens sat before him.

Charter's unblinking eyes stared down at them, disdain emanating from him. "Traitors!" He spat.

There was a roar of responses from the degenerates. Boos, hisses, and pleas mixed together in a cacophony of dissent.

"I swore no allegiance to *you*!" One bellowed.

Another cried, "I just wanted out of this hell!"

And yet another, "We want the surface; we want to be free!"

Charter's laugh started as a low chuckle, then grew to an echoing, bellowing laugh. Had he human eyes, they might have even teared up. The room grew uncomfortably silent.

Charter finished laughing and took a deep breath. With a sigh, he began, "My children, I am here to *save you*." He paused, then addressed the parishioners in the pews before him. "My loyal flock, my hive, raise your heads, come close and look upon the faces of these sons and daughters of Pelops. They wish to feed our children to the gods. Shall we, deified as we are, devour them instead?"

A haunting chant of agreeance came from the crowd of worshippers. He allowed them to hoop and holler, to get just riled up enough that some began to approach the pulpit, ready to devour those who, only hours before, they had called kin. One got close enough to the traitors that no Dutyman could stop her charge, and she ripped out a traitor's throat with her chelicerae in a bloody display that the chants only egged on. No traitor dared try to fight her off, in fear they might be next to receive that same, painful fate. Once she finished, Charter raised an arm to settle the crowd. Blood droplets decorated the base of the pulpit, and sticky viscera leaked down the center aisle between the pews.

"We should kill them, yes. In the past, this would have certainly been the way. But soon, we will ascend to a new era, a new way of being. Ours will be a pure civilization, one of peace as the gods intended. And so, we shall set these apostates free." There was a collective gasp of disgust from the bloodthirsty crowd and Charter let himself grin. *Oh, if only they knew. If only they knew of the horrifying fate awaiting those unprotected by the Magisters.* But he held his tongue. *All in due time.*

"Worry not," he said, in a soothing voice, "We shall remove all traces of our society from them. Their weapons and tools will be reclaimed, and their minds wiped. They will be released into the wild like the dumb beasts they are, and we will let our kin, and the cannibalistic nature of the earth take care of them. This is the declaration of the Grand Council of Magisters. For we are no longer of this place. We are destined for the stars!"

"We are destined for the stars!" Cried the congregation in response. They cheered as the traitors were led away by the Dutymen, whose mechanized arms and bodies moved almost robotically as they herded the defectors toward the surgical center. The parade of the unworthy was still in precession when Charter took his leave.

In his chambers, he raised a call to the Vice-Chancellor, a woman named Gregoria Spact, for the daily report. The comwindow chirped three times, then, with a flicker, Gregoria's perfectly insectoid face lit up the screen. He felt something stir deep within him as he gazed upon her majesty.

"Master Priest Charter," she said in her usual mechanically melodic tone.

"Your Excellency."

"Was the cleanse successful?"

"Yes, the hive surgeons are reverting the traitors as we speak."

"Wonderful. Accommodations have been made for your nest's departure to the ark in just a few days."

"Thank you, Excellency. We will begin preparations tonight after the evening sermon."

"You have served the Magisters well."

"I shall continue to do so, for as long as I am worthy."

"To the stars, Eloqueth." It was their order's usual farewell, but when she said it to him there was more than a note of familiarity. Even so, Gregoria did not often use his given name, as she was not prone to sentimentality. Today, despite her grainy, synthetic voice, he could hear some emotion in it. So he responded in kind.

"To the stars, Gregoria."

She smiled. Or, at least, he thought she smiled. It was hard to tell with her skin stretched out to accommodate the Arachnotech augmentations and ornate symbols of office that brought her so much closer to their exhaulted Arachnid overlords than he would ever be. After a lingering, affectionate silence, the comwindow flickered off.

Charter hung his vestments on the mannequin in his luxurious chambers, and took a seat at the desk to read through the material he had prepared for the coming sermon. Tonight would be the start of a new era for the collective, and he hoped it would bring peace, success, and glory to the Magisters and everyone involved in the hive. As he skimmed over his notes and The Manual, an alert flickered on his comwindow with a light chirp. With a glimpse, he could see that it was a message from the surface.

"Master Priest Charter, do you copy? Fuck! Hold on."

At first, pines danced against a fiery background where a speaker should be. Outcries and explosions echoed distantly among the static.

He heard the invisible speaker yell "Get down!" before a very intense explosion shook the earth hard enough to knock down the fieldcom. There was a brief burst of static as the feed was interrupted. For a moment, Charter thought the transmission would not revive. But then the comwindow came back online, and he was greeted with the noble, but grimy, countenance of a Battalion Commander.

"My apologies, Master Priest Charter. This is an urgent message."

"Go ahead, Commander." Charter did his best to keep a flat affect as the transmission shivered with each explosion. Dirt and viscera peppered the Commander's battle-worn uniform. The situation did not look good.

"We've run into a snag on our departure. Have you prepped your nest for leaving?"

"Not entirely, I--"

"Let me clarify. Could you leave tonight, if it was an emergency?"

"I suppose, if we--"

"Good, your new leave time is tomorrow morning at sunrise. Get your people to the site at least an hour before the sun comes up so we can get everyone into the craft."

"I don't understand; what's going on?"

The Commander was visibly irked by the question. "I suppose I should have introduced myself. My name is Commander Avarius, and I am calling you from what used to be the edge of your launch field. We are fighting off a massive force of Truydani supersoldiers, and we are barely able to hold them off. We will continue to defend this line until your departure, but we cannot keep Truydan at bay for much longer. There will not be another opportunity for you or your people to leave."

"I see..."

"I'll see you in a few hours, Priest."

"That's Master Priest--" But the transmission had already cut to static before he could correct the Commander.

His first task would be to call Vice-Chancellor Spact and confirm the information he'd just received. After that, there wasn't much time before the nest had to clear out entirely. This would mean leaving surgeons behind to finish off the rest of the traitors. Charter ground his fangs together as he dialed the Vice-Chancellor.

She answered in her nightgown, clearly half-asleep. "Eloqueth?" Her gritty voice was a soothing balm.

"Gregoria... ah, I mean, Vice-Chancellor Spact." His correction signaled to her the professional manner of the call and she shifted soberly in her seat, squaring her offset shoulders.

"Yes, Master Priest Charter? Are you encountering problems?"

"Something of the sort, yes. I've been informed that Truydan is encroaching on our launch field. Battalion Commander Avarius just radioed that we need to depart tomorrow at sunrise."

"The conditions will not be great for flying tomorrow," the Vice-Chancellor said, as though that were reason enough to put it off.

"Have you heard any of this news about Truydan?"

"No, I told my aide that I was not to be disturbed. I even turned off my comwindow."

Charter felt his blood run cold. "I'm intruding."

"No, you're not. This is important. I should have known

better; a Vice-Chancellor can't rest at such an important time as this."

"Gergoria, everyone needs a break sometimes." There was a pleasant pause, and he took in the subtle features of her gargantuan, inhuman smile.

"Honestly, I'm glad you called. I'll inform the others, assuming they haven't already been told of this development. As you know, project Veridian is our highest priority. If even one of the colonies is unable to convene with the rest of us up there, we'll feel that loss sorely for years to come. I wish you luck, Eloqueth, and I'll see you among the stars in just few weeks."

Charter stammered for a moment, fishing for words, any words, in any combination really, that would keep her on the line just a little longer. But there was nothing more to say except, "Right, good." He watched with some sort of unnamable sadness as she made ready to end the call. He didn't want her to go. He didn't want to wait weeks to see her face again.

At last his mind caught hold of something, and he leaned in toward the comwindow, close and quick. "Wait! Gregoria, if you turned off your receiver, how are we talking right now?" Had she made it so his calls would come through when no others could? Had she been expecting him to ring her in the middle of the night?

She looked up at him with an eerie bittersweetness, her sharp, bony finger a hair's breadth away from the button that would end the call. "It doesn't really matter much now, does it?"

There was something confirmatory in her voice, something he hadn't caught before. At last, he understood that his feelings for the Vice-Chancellor were requited. It was dangerous, and they both knew it. It also felt unavoidable, somehow. How strange that, in this world, they had helped build, *this* was the shred of humanity they had chosen to hold onto. Love, or lust, or something in between, was tucked safely away in their chests, hidden from the multitudinous eyes of the Magisters. The forbidden knowledge hung heavy and thick between them for a lingering moment.

"Gregoria--" Charter began, but he was interrupted by a heavy knock on the Vice-Chancellor's door.

"I am not to be disturbed," she said, flashing Charter what he read to be a waggish squint of her piercing eyes. But then the door opened with a heavy thud and Gregoria's face blanched.

"Gregoria, what's wrong?" Charter called into the com, but she did not respond to him.

"Get out of my office, you brute!" She bellowed, standing up now on her many legs, wings spread wide, thorax pumping with adrenaline. "I am warning you, I am not to be messed with."

"Gregoria, I'll radio for help!"

"It's too late, Eloqueth," she said, as much to herself as to him. Charter could see the hint of a stinger budding out from her quivering chest. There was poison there, enough to kill a human several times over. It would be just enough to take out the supersoldier, but it would end her life in the process. He knew that there was no saving her, and his heart shattered. Still, he could not look away.

There came a robotic chime that vaguely resembled a human language, and then a burst of fire, followed by the ghastly, defiant wail of Vice-Chancellor Gregoria Spact as she charged at the intruder, purple blood spewing from her bullet wounds as she moved. There was another bright burst of small explosions, followed by the heavy *clang,*

clang, clang, of supersoldier boots on the polished stone floor. In the background were the ragged gasps of the dying Vice-Chancellor.

"I'm so sorry my love," Charter muttered under his breath, then flicked the screen off before the Truydani warrior could see his face. Stomach swirling, he made a dash for his robes. It was time to leave.

Green light flashed in every corridor of the nest, and the dutiful citizens filed from their beds and workstations to the cathedral hall once more. There was no time to waste, so Master Priest Charter began his announcement before the pews were filled.

"This is an auspicious day, though it has come to us earlier than expected. Like thieves in the night, we shall steal away to the surface. You will not need to take any personal possessions, except your data chips. Everyone will follow me to the launch field where we shall face, together, our destiny." *Well, almost everyone,* he thought to himself. "The surgeons and those tasked with disposing of those we are casting out will join us after their tasks are complete."

It was a lie. It was a *necessary* lie. Many would be hesitant to leave without the surgeons who so dutifully maintained their augmentations. And there were, of course, the surgeons who might shirk their duties for the chance to fulfill the divine mission with the rest of the hive. But *their* divine duty was to remain behind, disassemble the traitors, and destroy any remaining tech that nonbelievers could steal and bastardize after the nest was abandoned. The plan had initially been to take them with everyone else after they fulfilled that part of their mission, which was no longer feasible.

"I know you've only just taken your seats, but it is now time to leave. We must move quickly, but with as much stealth as we can manage. The enemies are at our gates, trying to stop the inevitable." As if to punctuate his point, there was a rumble from the surface. "The Dutymen will guide you onward. For those of you just joining us, you will be informed of the news as we depart. Tonight, we move on toward our destiny. Tonight, we leave for the stars."

After a surprisingly enthusiastic cheer of *WE ARE DESTINED FOR THE STARS!*, the large crowd began filing out in the same way they had filed in. Orderly and calm, Aranchonech Cultists of all calibers and augmentations began the journey upward and outward from the nest. Master Priest gathered the Downpriests and Tyropriests together for a final meeting on how to proceed. The rectory was full to beyond capacity with hooded figures, silent as ghosts in the dim purple light cast by the moon through the stained glass dome.

"Brethren," he began, "today is a dark day. Our magnificent people are under atrocious attack by the Truydani supersoldiers, and I have reason to believe they've taken the west headquarters by force. After an urgent call from a Battalion Commander on the front lines, I reached out to Vice-Chancellor Spact to confirm our next moves. Instead of receiving new orders, I watched as she fought an Truydani soldier who had broken into the Vice-Chancellor quarters. She did not make it out alive.

"Time is of the essence, as their forces are closing in quick. We have until sunrise to depart, and we may have to do so without direct confirmation for lift-off from HQ. The risks here are considerable, and we will all be expected to make sacrifices worthy of the grand destiny we all share. I am counting on you to deliver our people to the stars."

Without waiting for confirmation, he donned his dark hood and stalked out of the room. His legs carried him above and around the crowd, so that he made it to the very front of the pack with ease. His timing could not have been better; they had just reached the opening to the nest. He insisted on being the first one out.

The night air was sticky and warm. Fireflies danced between trees as the crowd quietly made their way toward the orange glow in the distance. There was the stench of fire-scorched ocher spores. The fungus had become Truydan's weapon of choice over the recent decade. The Arachnotech Cultists were immune to the effects of the stuff, thanks to their augmentations and bio-engineering, but they were not immune to the stench of it. When it burned, it had the smell of necrosis and burning hair that no human nose could truly appreciate, augmentations or not.

It was that same stench which sat rank in the back of Charter's throat, mixing with the grief of watching Gregoria's final moments. He fought down the dismay that came with the thought that maybe Truydan would win and he would never make it off this planet. The ground shook beneath him as he led them over miles of terrain, occasionally glancing back to ensure they were keeping to the shadows of the treeline. And then they crested the final hill, just as the light of grey dawn was mixing with the red-orange smoke.

The scene would have been enough to bring Charter to his knees, but the weight of his station held him steady. He pressed onward, toward what he knew would be the most impossible task he could possibly face as a Master Priest. Ahead was Commander Avarius and the remainder of his forces – now a measly twenty or so Arachnotech warriors – defending the base of the shuttlecraft against nearly twice as many Truydani supersoldiers.

Charter stopped just before he would be visible from

the battlefield, and turned to his people. He faced them, knowing he would ask the impossible of them, and lowered his hood. As they gathered near and pressed in, he raised his voice only loud enough that he knew the soldiers below wouldn't catch on. The forest had nowhere near the acoustics of his cathedral, so he knew many of them would never feel the inspiration of his voice before what was likely to be their final duty, for the good of the nest.

"I am counting on those of you who can hear me to pass this message on to those in the back who cannot. The scene down there is grim at best. This is the final test of our faith before we can move onward to our divine and much-deserved future. Many of us will not make it. I am telling you this not to put fear into your hearts, but to free you from fear with the knowledge that your choices today will define our people for the rest of eternity. Regardless of whether you live or die, your actions will bring us all one step closer to our destiny among the stars."

Charter paused and looked over his flock, taking in the loyal faces one more time in the dim light of the imminent sunrise. "The Dutymen will hold off the Truydani forces as long as possible while we get the younglings onto the ship first, assembly-line style. Then whoever does not make it on before we succumb to the Supersoldiers will be charged with the task of ensuring liftoff conditions."

A swarm of disconcerted murmurs swept through the crowd as the message was passed on. Charter did his best to look stoic, despite his own certainty that none of them would make it out of this situation alive. He breathed and nodded his head in understanding. "This will be the hardest moment of your life. Remember our divine destiny as you draw their focus from our shuttle long enough for us to get into the air. If possible, get them close to the thrusters just before we ignite, and they will be burned to a crisp. If you survive the battle, your next task is to go to the closest nest, two-hundred miles west of here. You must warn them about Truydan's attempt to foil our plans. With luck, you'll be able to join their expedition."

He watched for a moment as fear and acceptance swept through his followers. Then, he turned toward the ridge and pulled the hood back over his head. He had expected, and maybe even secretly hoped for, pushback. Instead, there was nothing but the sound of his flock steeling themselves to face their imminent deaths for the sake of a fortunate few from their ranks.

After a few moments, all the youths had been ushered to the center-front of the crowd, a few priests accompanying the smaller ones who might have a hard time keeping up. The Dutymen lined the perimeter of the tightly-bunched group. Master Priest Charter watched the fight below them from a few meters off, accompanied by a Tyropriest named Jessup Elerias who had often bested him at Cheops. Elerias was his star pupil. She was going to be his next inductee into True Priesthood. Her induction would have happened when they reached the first waystation, at Mars; the journey there would have supplied them with plenty of time to strengthen and train her mind for the transition.

Charter waited until she finished her suggestion on how to approach the coming conflict, then placed a hand on her shoulder. Before he could speak, she leaned in and hugged him.

"Master Priest Charter, it has been an honor studying under you." She spoke the words as though they were a valediction.

"Tyropriest Elerias, I–"

Before Charter could speak possibly the only

sentimental words he'd ever deigned to utter, a barrage of bolter fire rained down on the pair. He dove down with a sharp shout, long appendages sprawling out to shelter his dear pupil, who lay face down behind a nearby boulder. His flock was still hidden amongst the trees, but he knew by the sound of thudding footsteps making their way up the steep basin ridge that their cover would be blown in a matter of minutes.

"Elerias, we need to move. Now!" He did not bother whispering anymore. They had been found.

The Tyropriest did not respond beyond a gurgling, choking breath. Her warm blood pooled beneath her, soaking her robes and the ground. It wasn't long before Charter's bonespire arms were coated with the congealing wetness. With a single, sweeping motion, he stood and scooped her cooling carcass up and tucked it into the nearby brush. Her crumpled body was a heap of unlivable geometry and tattered flesh, and it crunched when he moved it. It didn't take a medical specialist to know that she would die soon if she was not already lost. Shots buzzed past him, each one missing his bony arms or bulbous face by only a hair's breadth. Ignoring them, he gestured to his flock to get ready for a race to their destiny.

"The time has come! On my mark," He couldn't quell the quiver in his voice. The sensation of tear production burned at phantom nerves where his eyes used to be.

Master Priests are not built for battle. Their augmentations are useful for sensing the inner thoughts of followers, for orating to the masses, for inspiring useful actions among congregants who might otherwise stray from the destiny they all had to earn together. But Master Priests *are* designed to lead, and Master Priest Charter applied that knowledge to his nest's predicament on the ridge. Another volley of fire hummed by him, and he fought the sudden urge to wet himself.

Dignity, he thought to himself, *one display of fear, and we'll never make it onto that damned ship.* Risen now to his full height, Charter turned toward the super-soldiers running at him from below, and steeled himself against the unbearably human urge to run and hide. With what he hoped was an inspiring glance to the huddled mass of refugees he'd cared for since his induction into the priesthood, he gave the command.

"To the stars!"

The group charged out of the trees and down into the basin with an enthusiastic shout. The Dutymen were first to clash with the Truydani abominations halfway down the steep ridge. Arachnotech Cultists rained down around them, bolstering their defense with sweeps of various mechanized augmentations in the form of serrated digging trowels, drill bits, and lasers calibrated for carving into bedrock. None of them were any kind of real match for the super-soldiers, who hacked, and carved, and blew their way through the cultists with almost comical ease. Still, the sheer quantity of targets seemed to slow the soldiers down enough to aid Charter's escape with the younglings.

Towering above them, children and priests sheltered beneath him like eggs to a mother hen, Charter made a beeline for the shuttlecraft, which seemed remarkably unharmed despite the ongoing battle. Commander Avarius, however, looked much worse for wear. Avarius, now one of only two troops fending off enemies from the base of the craft, cut down an Truydani soldier who had lost their helmet. He did so with an exhausted, hacking motion of his sword, then locked eyes with Charter, ignoring the spray of blood that speckled his own dirty face in the burgeoning gold of dawn.

It looked like Avarius shouted something before he turned away and shot at another soldier, but the noise of the skirmish was too loud for Charter to know what was said. He was still about 20 meters from the craft, when Avarius fell to his knees, ruined by the single thrust of an Truydani soldier's blade into his chest. At the moment of realization that this was, indeed, the end, his face showed neither surprise, nor fear. Instead, his tired features were layered with a sort of sad acceptance and relief. He lingered there a moment, watching as Charter reached the entry portal to the ship loaded the younglings onto the craft in squirming handfuls against a backdrop of fire and spores and cultists somehow winning against the overpowered Truydani forces on the ridge.

Charter kept his gaze while Avarius gave in to the weight of death, falling sidelong to the ground and throwing up a puff of orange spores and ash. It had only been a few minutes since they had crested the ridge, but Charter had felt himself age a lifetime in those impossible moments. He helped the other priests onto the ship as a small group of Dutymen fought off the remaining Truydani super-soldiers who surrounded the craft, then turned to survey who was left of his flock.

What he saw was promising. About 30% of his nest remained in working condition, which was more than he had expected to survive against the Truydani soldiers. *Avarius must have given them one hell of a fight.* Charter waved to them in an effort to call them closer to the shuttle. Some would have to remain behind and keep the Truydani soldiers from downing the shuttle as it lifted off and passed into the sky, but the ones who got to him first would be loaded onto the ship.

But none of them would make it to the ship. As he helped the last priest up and waited for the first of the retreating cultists to make it within his arm's reach, a thundering explosion broke against the sky. Truydan had sent reinforcements in the form of aircraft. The use of birds of prey was a somewhat new development in Truydan's approach to the war between the two powers, which they had begun to employ more frequently in an attempt to stop the mass exodus of Arachnotech Cultists that had been slowly taking place for the past three years.

Master Priest Charter, and surely most if not all of his flock, had been born well after the gods had touched down on Earth. Being unaccustomed to the haunting noise of aircraft, they all looked to the sky to identify the source of the sound. That brief pause was all the gunner needed to mow down nearly half the survivors. Charter watched as uncountable shots from the unseen wraith blasted his followers into pink mist on the dawn breeze. Then, before he could meet the same fate, he bounded into the shuttle's entrance and bolted the door shut.

"Tyropriest Nepper, get us out of here!"

"What about the others?" Someone asked.

"Initiating launch," Nepper announced.

"It's now or never. Truydan sent sky-guns," Charter replied into the dark, strapping himself in. "Are the children secured?"

"Five seconds," Nepper said.

"They're all set," another priest said.

Charter's head swam. They were headed into the void without a full crew. With the arrival of the sky-gun, he knew there would be no survivors left on the ground to reconvene with on Mars, if they even made it that far. They were aboard a ship meant to carry, and be manned by, an entire nest. Well over half of the nearly fifty who had made it aboard were younglings. And a third of those had only basic youth augmetics. As the ship rumbled its ascent and rounds from the Truydani sky-gun began to meld with the white noise of atmosphere bouncing off the spacecraft's hull, Charter contemplated the survival of his nest, which had been effectively pruned to less than one-tenth of its original size.

Artificial gravity locked in as they left Earth's orbit and pulled into the swirling freefall of the void. Master Priest Charter had finally taken his place among the stars, but at what cost? He unstrapped himself from his seat and commanded all priests not dedicated to flying the shuttlecraft to help him conduct a security sweep through the whole ship. Two priests resolved to take shifts flying and sweeping, so both could get the lay of the place, and neither would get too tired guiding the behemoth through the black.

They had no Dutymen to protect them, but Charter had access to every part of the ship, including weapons stores. His first stop was the armory. Each of the nine priests below him held a weapon for the first time that day. Charter could not use a firearm, for obvious reasons, but he had been trained in the basic use of these types of guns prior to his priesthood, as he had been born on the Orange Frontier. So he taught the younger priests how to turn the weapons on, how to aim them, how to shoot.

He hoped none of them would need to use that knowledge, especially the Downpriests, who had never regained their sight after they failed their True Priest trials and would likely miss whatever target they might shoot at. The chances of a stowaway being anyone other than an

Truydani Supersoldier were slim to none. The priests were no match for Truydan's mutated experiments. He resolved to train them all in finding and hitting targets over the next seven months they were to travel together in the great vacuum, provided they survived this security sweep.

It took six hours to check the entire place, and even then Charter was unsure if every single nook and cranny had been inspected. As far as they all could tell, there were no unwanted visitors aboard their new home. The eight lower priests who were not piloting the craft convened with Charter outside the armory to return their weapons. The air around them was heavy with sorrow, so the Master Priest moved to speak. He intended to rouse them, but what came out only served to sustain their weariness.

"Our duty is to the younglings, now. Our duty is to *their* destinies, not ours," Charter started, taking a sermonic tone. But when he found that he had more to say but not the words to say it, he sighed and rested his feet on the metal deck for the first time since he'd left his seat. His arms folded up like angel wings behind him, and he bowed his head.

For a moment, he let the pain of loss wash over him. *Gregoria. Elarias. Avarius. Countless others.* He saw their faces in his mind's eye in striking detail. He savored the pain of the fresh wounds burned into his brain because he knew, in time, the pain would fade along with their memories. Then, rage boiled up and overtook the sadness.

He saw the demonic visages of the supersoldiers who had killed his flock. His family. He didn't have to think hard to remember those details, which were the same on every Truydani helm. Every one of them hid behind a dower, expressionless mask. Not human, not insectoid, nothing holy there. Only void, mechanical anonymity. Freedom from the guilt of slaughter, if they were even capable of guilt.

And then he remembered the priests around him, waiting for him to continue. "Sometimes," he said, looking up, "there are no words for the things we must do." And with that, he left for his chambers to meditate on a plan.

The solution ended up being a simple one. After reading several manuals on long-distance communication in the form of "video kites" with the sole remaining Vice-Chancellor, Viktor Esparagae, Master Priest Charter gave the orders for all children to be put into hypersleep. The priests would be in charge of running the ship, which, after some reconfiguring, would only require monitoring of some autopilot protocol and response to any emergency alerts. It would be almost eight months until they reached Mars, and Master Priest Charter intended to spend the majority of that time in meditation over the atonement for the actions he took as a leader which ended up in the destruction of his nest.

Communications with Vice-Chancellor Esparagae would reveal that Truydan had leveraged an attack on a plethora of launch sites and nests, including the Magisters' Headquarters, and Charter was one of the few who had made it into the air that day. Still, they were pressing forward with project Veridian as before. As a positive, Charter's medical specialists who had remained behind were able to reclaim many tools from the battlefield after the Truydani troops were finished there.

"It seemed as though Truydan had no desire to harvest or scavenge any of our tech. I had your surgeons take the usable parts to the nearest nest. They'll arrive at Mars about a year behind you." There was a tense optimism to Esparagae's voice that Charter couldn't quite place. He would never get the chance to ask about it, because five months into Charter's journey, Esparagae's shuttlecraft exploded in Earth's atmosphere, killing the only remaining Vice-Chancellor and his pupils.

The same day they received the kite detailing Vice-Chancellor Esparagae's death was the same day Charter received an urgent kite from the Magisters themselves. The notification came in halfway through his reading of the detailed report of Esparagae's tenure as Vice-Chancellor. At first, he thought he misread the notification. But it flashed purple on his screen, demanding to be opened before he could use the comwindow for anything else.

So he clicked it, unaware that his life was about to change in a way he never thought possible. The Magisters never communicated via video, and they were notoriously concise. They could not use human speech, the capability having been removed by the many complicated procedures performed on them to remake them as close to gods as possible. This was likely due to the fact that they dictated in a sort of click-tap-code. Their aids typed up confidential letters that were sent directly to the person they were intended for, and copies were never made. Once a Magister approved and sealed something written by a scribe, it was considered living, breathing truth. Charter tapped the notification on the comwindow and a short block of script filled the small screen.

"Written by the scribes of The Magisters of the Arachnotech.

Ordained only for the eyes of Master Priest Eloqueth Charter.

Regarding: Ascension.

Master Priest Eloqueth Charter, you are

hereby commanded to ascend to the new role of Vice-Chancellor. Conduct the proper ceremony with the priests aboard your vessel, and you will hold the title in a temporary capacity until you receive the rights of transition at the surgical center on Mars. This message has received the approval and seal of Magister Bell."

There was no questioning the will or intentions of the Magisters. Still, Charter had to fight the urge to respond to the message with the one question that buzzed around his mind like an angry hornet. *Why?* Why him? Why now? Sure, Esparagae was dead, and his pupils too, but Charter was hardly qualified for such a job. He had received no formal training. He had read through the ritual for ascension to the Vice-Chancellorship once, maybe twice. It was not even considered a natural progression from his current position as Master Priest.

But the word of the Magisters was living, breathing truth. He had to do as he was commanded. So he called his priests away from their stations and meditations to make the solemn announcement. He did his best to make it clear that he did not want the new designation, that he had not asked for it, nor did he feel he deserved it. It was Tyropriest Angus Lostlight who put an end to Charter's lengthy protestations.

"--But the Magisters said you are to fill the role of Vice-Chancellor?" Lostlight interrupted.

"Yes," Charter said hesitantly.

"Then we will not go against their will by helping you find a way out of this, though it seems from what you've said that you'd rather die than move into your new role. We do not get to decide the time of our death." The others nodded in agreement. "They must have found you worthy in one way or another."

"Or they're just short on people," Charter said, immediately regretting his candid bitterness.

"Stagnation is death, Master Priest Charter. You cannot remain in your position any longer. We'll perform the ritual in twelve hours. We need some time to prepare and find substitutions for the things we don't have on hand."

Charter nodded and sighed. "You are good priests who understand your duties perhaps better than I do. So then there comes the task of designating a new Master Priest for our nest," Charter said, looking around the room. "Some of you have been training for the trials of the True Priesthood. I will take you under my wing for the remainder of our journey. When we land on Mars, you will begin your transition."

Most of the ship had been sealed off by bulkheads to limit the amount of work needed to maintain it. Of the rooms that remained available for use were the priests' quarters, the hypersleep chamber, the mess hall, the head, the cockpit, and the temple. The latter is where the ritual would take place. It was a large room with obsidian black walls that blended in with the bay windows that showed a clear display of the void outside and the celestial bodies that speckled it with light.

In one corner, near the pulpit, was a votive where a candle burned for each one of the dead lost that day on the battlefield. And Vice-Chancellor Spact. Charter had spent the majority of their trip in the temple, meditating, praying, delivering sermons, conducting rituals with the lower priests at the designated times. Most often, though, he was kneeling at the base of the altar to their gods, contemplating the possible milestones in his path along the ascent to perfection among the stars. Never once had he considered the bend he was about to round.

Vice-Chancellorship was for chosen ones; it was for the Magisters' favored pupils, not for Master Priests. Yet, when he entered the fane for the first time since receiving the message from the Magisters, he felt the rightness of it settle upon him. The space was decorated specially for the occasion. Red silk hung from the ceiling in the corners of the room. The pews had been stowed, the spaces where the rows had been were now marked with tall, white candles, intricately carved with runic inscriptions. The old votive candles had been replaced with fresh ones that stood tall and free of wax drippings. Gold fabric delineated a circle at the center of the room, where the floor carvings created a shallow trough in the interconnected shape of the solar system, complete with the Sun, planets, and the larger moons.

Charter wore a white robe fringed with gold trim and tassels on the sleeves the lower priests had fashioned out of a set of the ship's curtains. The fabric was just this side of sheer, and his skin prickled beneath it against the chill of the recycled air. The Tyropriests and Downpriests waited for him in the dim room, dark robes barely visible in the candlelight. As Charter entered, on his feet, through the parishioners' doorway, Tyropriest Lostlight descended the stairs from the pulpit. Lostlight raised his arms and the other six priests turned to face the center of the circle.

Lostlight's voice boomed across the amphitheater. "Master Priest Eloqueth Charter, the Magisters have seen fit to elevate you to the office of Vice-Chancellor. Are you worthy of this station?"

No, Charter thought. But he didn't say it. He had studied the script. He knew the words. "The Magisters have deemed me worthy of my next station." Charter padded, barefoot, arms folded up behind him, to the edge of the circle of hooded priests.

"Are you ready to receive this sentence of servitude to the gods and our great destiny among the stars?"

No. But again, Charter spoke only the words on the script, hoping they would endear themselves to his heart before the ritual's end. "I humbly accept the duty I am charged with and await my impending transition. Through my pain and evolution, there will be hope and a future for all our kind."

The next step in the ritual would be complicated. They needed a blood sacrifice. A *human* blood sacrifice. Traditionally, this role fell to a single volunteer from the nest who had chosen to remain purely human for such ritualistic purposes. The human would be bled out and left as an offering to their arachnid deities. But aboard the ship, in the middle of space, weeks away from Mars and months away from Earth, there were only priests and younglings on board. Still, a sacrifice had to be made. Even if the gods were not here to consume the results of it.

Lostlight spoke again, this time a tone of restrained emotion staining his voice. "We present the offering, that the gods may be appeased by this, the Magisters' will."

The soft glow of a small candle emerged from behind Lostlight. The gold flicker illuminated the edges of the white robe of a Downpriest, their face shrouded beneath the darkness of their hood. Charter stepped to the center of the circle as the faceless priest stopped at the shallow part of the trough in the floor. Lostlight stood beside the Downpriest and continued the ritual.

"Do you, humble human, offer your body as sacrifice to

the gods? Pure as you are, knowing your destiny is to serve them among the stars?"

"I do." The raspy voice of the Downpriest, who had barely spoken a hundred words since his trials, raked like gravel over Charter's heart.

"Kneel," Lostlight said, pulling a dagger from his robe.

The Downpriest dropped smoothly to his knees, leaning over the trough in wordless prayer. His face was serene, even as the cool knife ripped open the flesh of his neck, and his life blood spilled out into the trough. It flowed to all the planets depicted in the inlaid solar system there, filling the deepest bowl, the sun, at Charter's feet. He waited until his soles were coated in the warm stuff, then scooped it awkwardly with his inhuman hands to paint it on his chest in the shape of eight legs. It smelled sweetly of warm iron. He painted his lips with it, drawing two lines down from the corners of his mouth, like mandibles. He tasted the salt of it on his tongue. This was the food of the gods. Soon, he would even more closely resemble the gods more ways than he knew how to count, and this would become a normal part of his diet. He shuddered to think about it, but whether it was out of disgust or excitement, he couldn't tell.

Lostlight held the deflating Downpriest in place as the warm fluid spurted out. "You have done the greatest service you could have ever performed, Downpriest. Charter, take this sanctified offering to the gods, and your ritual will be complete."

There was no natural feature where they could leave the body as an offering to their Arachnid overlords, so Charter and the others dragged the carcass to the airlock at the rear end of the ship. It was surreal to walk past all the bulkheads which had been closed for months, very much like traveling into a strange wilderness. The floor and walls were especially cold, smelling of icy metal and moonlight instead of the same stale recycled air. Charter's footprints and small droplets from the Downpriest breadcrumbed their path past ghost town medbays and living quarters with doors sealed like mausoleums.

The airlock was simple enough to use. They placed the stiffening Downpriest in the offering position, and Charter performed the last rite over the corpse, committing him to his destiny as a servant to the gods. Then, they left the airlock and sealed it. Charter pressed a few buttons, and after a countdown and a warning klaxon, the Downpriest was out amongst the celestial bodies, the first offering to the gods to ever be delivered into the black. Just like that, their crew was down to seven priests and once Vice-Chancellor.

Mars was well in view, and so was Charter's destiny... as a god, in the making.

8

REMAINDER OF THE DAY

JB LETTERCAST

Three of Five

THREE SUPERSOLDIERS SIT around a table in the dim mess hall of a Truydani spaceship en route to the Arachno-cultist colony on Mars. One, a man named Duff, stares off into the distance and runs a tired hand through his prematurely gray hair. Another, Bran, smashes reconstituted vegetable matter with his fork, frustration creasing his scarred face. The third, Avery, hastily scarfs her food, glancing around anxiously between shoveled scoops of the unsavory stuff as though a hungry bird or sneaky vermin might steal it right off her plate.

None of them should be there. All of them should be dead on Earth, buried under the tons of rubble that used to be Chancellor City. Instead, they're eating dinner, surrounded by others who look just like them; gray travel sweats, short, tapered haircuts, grotesquely rippling muscles, scars decorating almost every inch of exposed flesh.

But appearance and substance are two different things.

These people look like them, smell like them, talk like them. But these people are only that: similar. Fewer than one-third of the soldiers aboard the craft are survivors of the impossible battle, the *Final* Battle, which Earth had just borne painful witness to.

The names of their deceased and missing brethren are still being listed in monotonous litany over the intercom, even as they pass into their third Earth-day of travel to raze the red planet. Life goes on, even with the very essence of death haunting the recycled air. This was the plan all along. Crewmembers perform their tasks, supersoldiers prepare to go into hyper-sleep, the lights cycle day and night in the hab bay, and mess is churned out at its usual times.

All the while, the three await their turn in the hyper-pods. They were not supposed to make it out alive. They must be medically and psychologically approved before joining the ranks of those preparing to be dispatched against the enemy forces nestled in the rust-red barren wasteland of Mars.

Avery, Duff, and Bran are some of the very few survivors of the Last Battle. It is called that for its being the last battle that could have ever been waged on Earth. Survivors, which are serving out mandated leave time, are being evaluated last.

They have all been assigned a group number and encouraged to bond with their group members as a part of the process. The numbers were chosen using an algorithm designed to put the soldiers into spaces with people they know or who are at least similar to them. They have no other duties but to train, talk, and show up on time to all their appointments. But Truydani soldiers are built to fight, kill, and keep moving. For them, the waiting is almost painful.

"I just want to kill something," Avery says, chasing her final mouthful with a gulp of water.

"Nothing to kill in here," Bran says, stabbing his protein slab for emphasis, "even the meat was never really alive." He hoists it in the air dramatically and takes a grimacing bite.

"We can go to the training cages," Duff offers, pushing his tray away and leaning forward on his elbows.

"Beats sitting around in this stinky place," Avery replies, already standing to leave.

"Yeah, like the gym smells any better," Duff says, following after her.

"At least the gym is *supposed* to smell like ass," Bran says. The hint of a chuckle that plays at the end of his sentence is swallowed immediately by the crushing pain of sorrow. Xavier would have come back at him with some smart remark. Instead, only silence fills the vacant space where his dearest companion used to live.

At the cages, Avery selects her weapons. Bran sits to the side as referee between her and Duff. Sparring matches go quick with Avery, who is arguably the best out of any of them at one-on-one combat.

Though she's never spoken it aloud, Avery classifies herself as a warrior instead of a soldier. She has no need to fight battles alongside brothers-in-arms. Why should she? She can slip in unnoticed and win a war single-handedly while the others play political games and run strategic gambits. She can topple an empire by removing a single stone from its foundation while everyone else keeps each other distracted.

Avery believes she can slay any foe as long as she knows its weakness. She strikes swiftly, her blows pointed and precise. She gets the job done with little mess or noise. Just a blink, just a flash, and it's over, and she emerges triumphant, knowing she's finished the job. But this did not happen during the Last Battle.

During the Last Battle, she had failed to remove the all-important stone from the Arachno-cultist foundation. She had floundered, flabbergasted when things did not go according to plan. Her intel was wrong, and she failed to intuit it. She, death's favored silent warrior, had lost. And while the only audience to her failure was herself, she knows it to be the most devastating failure of her career.

Reminded of her shame and anger, she flings an array of sharp throwing knives in Duff's direction, which he barely dodges. She watches as one clips him and draws a droplet of dark red blood from his shoulder. "Let's fight already."

Duff swipes the blood away and levels his battleax toward her. "Yes, let's."

Bran watches as the two dance around the cage. Duff employs the usual tactics he's used since they were boys in training. Duff has never been the best at single combat, but he can get the job done. He knocks Avery on her back and pins her with the blade of his ax, and Bran calls a reset. "One point, Duff."

Duff's area of excellence is in flying. He was born to be a pilot. This is why Duff and Bran were separated early in their training. Duff managed to escape the fate of his and Bran's classmates, which was to become cannon fodder for Truydan. He was pleasantly surprised when, nearly a decade later, they reunited in the supersoldier program, each with exciting new stories to tell. Bran introduced Duff to Jindra, and Duff introduced Bran to Xavier. The four of them made quite the team.

They would all meet Avery at one of their first assignments as supersoldiers, eventually earning her respect over the course of a year of intense missions together. Others, too, had been a part of that tight-knit group, but in the end, only the five of them stayed alive and in touch. They would often meet up and trade stories of honor and glory long after their more youthful days – and scores of brethren – had passed on.

Eventually, Duff and Jindra developed a unique, intimate closeness not often seen among Truydan's bioenhanced ranks. They were never officially an item, but their passion for each other was only ever paralleled by their brutal skill as an Arachnodrone-killing team. Similar could be said for Bran and Xavier, who excelled at dispatching any living thing that crawled upon the earth – especially bugs.

But none of these five will ever again sit around a fire with all the others, telling stories late into the night. Xavier and Jindra lie lifeless upon the mass grave that was once Earth. It is impossible for the remaining three not to feel that their own souls were laid to rest alongside their comrades.

As the fourth round begins with Avery taking her inevitable lead against Duff and Bran tallying up the hits, they know that when the next chime sings, they must sit down and tell the stories they do not want to tell. They will sit in a chair across from some doctor who cannot possibly know them or even begin to see the world through their lens and tell the gut-wrenching tale of how they survived. No hot fire and roasted locust, no jibes from Xavier nor cheering from Jindra; just an unfeeling AI therapist and the cold, clinical examination room.

Clinical Record 16895: Duff MacGarvey

We waited longer than we should have. Bran's locator blinked on at the last moment, and I couldn't bring myself to leave just yet. There was time. Not much, but some. Enough, maybe, for Bran and anyone else to come aboard. So I waited, willing the little dot on the screen to move faster. At this rate, we'd have to leave him behind. I wondered how many of our people survived the battle. Our birds were designed to take at least twenty apiece, but so far, my hold only had six.

"It's past time to go," someone called from the passenger compartment. I didn't recognize their voice. Our forces had multiplied to nearly thirty thousand over the past decade. He either came from somewhere I'd never been, or he maybe was new. I made a mental note to learn his name and rank once we made it into the air.

"I'm the pilot. I say when it's time to go." I didn't take my eyes off Bran's red dot. There was the sound of another soldier hurling himself into my craft. The metal scraped as he slid along the floor, twisted, and blasted an Augment to smithereens. "Better not scuff up my ship," I said. It was a half-hearted attempt at a joke.

"You're not still supposed to be here," the seventh passenger said, breathless.

"That's a damned poor way to say thank you!" I turned around at the familiar voice and reached my hand out to help Jindra up off the floor. "For the Glory!" I cheered, clapping her hand in mine.

Jindra locked eyes with me as she stood, glancing warily out the hatch. "For Humankind!" She responded, eye glinting with something akin to mischief. We embraced, and she pulled off her helmet. "Why are you still on the ground, Duff? Something wrong with the bird?"

"No. Waiting for Bran."

Her eyes glanced over to the display where Bran's beacon showed his approach nearing only five blocks away. "There's plenty more of us out there without beacons, Duff."

"All the more reason to stay," I said, leading her to the cockpit.

She shook her head and sighed knowingly. Sweat droplets soaked her locs. "We knew this was a suicide mission." She paused to scratch some blood off the barrel of her bolter before tucking it in the thigh holster. "We were the decoys, the bait. It's our job to distract them. It's your job to get the survivors out alive. These soldiers in here did their job, and they made it out alive. They depend on you to carry them the rest of the way."

She was right. Bran was four blocks shy of making it out alive, but time had run out. I sat in the pilot's chair and pressed the button to close the rear hatch. "Everyone, strap in; we're leaving. I stopped Jindra when she moved to take her seat in the rear with the others. "Lost my gunner. You good to stand in?"

Jindra nodded and sat beside me in the co-pilot's seat, looking solemn. "I'm sorry, Duff. This was messier than anyone wanted it to be."

"Speaking of–" I said, pointing to an alert that just popped up on the dashboard.

"Is that the Commander?" She asked.

"And... the Chancellor?"

An uncanny voice came from the monitor. "*We shall ascend, and you will belong to the worms.*"

"Is it... speaking?" I asked. But before Jindra could

answer, there was the sound of a loud *BANG!* and the Commander cried out in horror, scrambling toward us from the screen. He strained against the many arms of his captors, mouth gaping as if to say something, anything at all – and the image went to snow.

Through the haze of static, we heard the Commander cry out two words:

TAKE COVER!

... I gunned it. I disobeyed the order, even as I saw the Shatterer streaming toward us like a comet. It was so bright I could barely see and so hot it confused my instruments. I dropped the bird near where I hoped Bran and Xavier were and threw open the hatch. The soldiers in my hold were screaming at me.

Jindra was screaming, too. Hers are the only words I remember now.

"Goddamn it, Duff, you idiot!" And then she hurled herself out the back hatch to find our friends. I could barely hear her call back from outside the craft, "I love you!" We never said it into the comm beads.

I didn't want her to go out there. I had planned to send someone else or go myself to find them, but she just... went. She was always like that, brave and thick-headed. She probably even knew I would have gone out there myself, and she didn't even give me an option. Mere moments passed like hours until, eventually, two figures stumbled clumsily into the hatch. We had mere seconds left before we needed to be far away from where we were when Jindra's voice buzzed in on my comms.

"Duff... I can't find them anywhere, but I–" static cut her off.

"They're in the craft, Jindra; come back!"

"--a pack of bugs, I'm not going to make it–" she

grunted, followed by the sound of her chainsword grinding as it sliced through something sinewy and hit concrete.

"Jindra? Jindra!" I was frantic. I'm never frantic. The soldiers behind me were about to pull me out of the pilot seat and try to fly the damned thing themselves. We were officially out of time. I unbuckled myself and made to stand, to fight them off or maybe to just let them have it and find a different way to save Jindra. But as I opened my mouth to command Bran to take command, her voice came in again. It was crystal clear and calm.

She was always the perfect antithesis of me. Strong, contrary, brave.

"Duff, go. Now." It was an order from someone I now understand to be the only person I had ever given any real power over me in my life.

"I love you," I said. There was no reply, only fading static as I thrust us up into the atmosphere with impossible speed, riding the edge of the first powerful shockwave emanating from the cultist's mega bomb.

It was going to be a bumpy ride.

Clinical Record 18843: Bran Halloway

"Xavier! We have to go. Now!" I threw my busted bolter into the nearest slag pile and turned on my locator beacon. We'd been had. Time to get out while we still had the chance. Just to our right was a clear enough path in the right direction. I scrambled over a pile of rubble and reached down to pull him up.

"You go. I'll catch up!" Xavier always had to be the hero. Even as we retreated through the ancient city ruins, he found new, exciting ways to one-up our enemies. At that very moment, he was using a rusty piece of rebar to bash and stab at our pursuers. "They're leaving *now*, whether we're on that ship or not," I urged him. As if to amplify my point, the deafening rumble of spacecraft engines shook the crumbled walls around us and tossed a new veil of superfine concrete-gypsum ash into the air.

Perfect.

I grabbed Xavier by the shoulder and pulled. He protested at first until he saw that the dust had congealed to form a sort of haze we could escape into. He nodded and dropped the rebar. And then we ran.

The grips of our metal shoes tore holes in the tired asphalt. The inside of my visor glistened with condensation from my sweat and breath, but I could still see the map clearly enough to get us there. We took a left. The roof of the craft towered in the distance, wavering in the heat like a mirage.

"Four more blocks!" My voice came out mute against the whining howl of the craft. I'd been yelling for days now as my company fought our way through that maze of ruins the Magisters called "Chancellor City." We had been a necessary distraction for their security forces while another group took care of their leaders, but the job was done, and it was time to get off the planet. Someone had to live on to make the sacrifices worth the blood they spilled. I was going to be that someone.

Then, for the first time since we'd lost contact with the rest of our unit, my radio crackled to life.

I managed to make out two words through the static before the world went black.

TAKE COVER!

Something massive blotted out the sun, then lit up the sky. Everything, the ground, the rubble, the bugs, Xavier, turned to alabaster and onyx, and a supersonic roar filled the air, rattling my suit and overcoming the noise-suppressors on my helm. Against the backdrop of pearlescence, the pitch-black speck that was supposed to be our ride lifted up and sped off into the sky.

"Fantastic," I said to myself as much to my partner. "Well, that's it, I suppose. Do you think we have time for a drink before that thing hits?" But when I glanced back, Xavier was not with me.

Amidst the shortening shadows, I saw something moving under the rubble. "Xav, is that you?"

There was no reply.

"I've got visual on... on something. Might be a bug, I don't know." I checked my gun – out of charge. Scanning the area, I saw what looked like a chainsword half-buried in the slag, but pulling it out would mean turning my back on whatever was emerging from the recrement. The options were either to risk dying with my back to a potential enemy, or to die without ever having had a chance to fight it off. It was an easy choice. "Xav? I see a chainsword; I'm going to grab it and hope it has power."

I scrambled over small concrete piles and gripped the hilt with both hands. As I began to pull, I could feel the servo-motorized joints whir into overdrive. The pile on it must have weighed tons because even my suit, which was built to handle enormous stress, was beginning to struggle. A green light flashed furiously at the top right corner of my helm screen. There was movement behind me. The death scream of the incoming Shatterer had broken my helm's external audio processors. My eardrums popped, and the world became mute.

"Come on..." I switched tac, pushed on the hilt, and dislodged the weapon just enough. Some chunks of debris fell, and I pulled back again, hard, wiggling it left and right as I went, and the chainsword finally came free. Without looking, I used its inertia to swing it up and around in a wide arc, flicking the ignition switch off and on again in a desperate attempt to start what was likely a dead weapon.

It felt like slow motion. The engine had not engaged by the time I reached the peak of my swing, so I flipped the switch off and on one more time, knowing that even if the weapon did not turn on, it would still do some damage to whatever had just sprung up behind me. I willed it to power on, now on the verge of connecting with the target – which I still had yet to lay eyes on. Off. Slight pause. On.

A familiar vibration shook my fingers as it rumbled to life, the engine's noise unable to compete with the muffled but ear-bursting noise of the Shatterer, which loomed ever more brightly over my head. The blade connected less than half a moment later, sawing down into the flesh of... of what?

For a moment, I was mortified. The scuffed and dusty orange of a shoulder guard glinted at me in the painful light. The number was familiar – it was Xavier's. My heart sank as I realized that the unforgivable had happened – the beast whose maw I was slicing into even as it bent over to devour me had eaten Xavier.

How had I not even noticed?

Then, a shadow fell, dark and fast. At first, I thought it was a preeminent blast cloud emanating from the Shatterer, which was scorchingly close to impact. Piles of stone, brick, and concrete collapsed around me, crushing the bastard bug in front of me and pulling me under like the rip current from a tidal wave.

I let the current take me, hoping for a swift end. Instead, I found myself somehow resurfaced by the flow of rubble as it slid down the unkempt streets of the demolished city. As I was thrust from utter blackness into the bright light, I saw a hand reaching out for help. I hoped it was Xavier. I prayed to I-don't-even-know-who that he had somehow freed himself from the Arachnid and maybe even been the source of that tower's demise.

Even as the rise still churned and settled, I pulled myself out of the piles and scrambled across the top of the flow until I reached the hand. I hoped it was attached to a body – to Xavier's body, preferable. I hoped whoever it was connected to was alive and not ground to a pulp. As I dug them out of their potential grave, I already knew in my soul that it could not possibly be my partner. This person wore special issue armor – at least it looked that way from what had been left on them after their tumble through the tower.

"Can you hear me?" I asked, calling on all channels. "Are you alright?"

Suddenly, Bran's voice came through. "You have ten seconds to get in."

Clinical Record 12037: Avery [REDACTED]

> *Clinician's note:*
>
> *The following record has been sanitized per protocol.*

Truydan loved its soldiers. It loved some of us so much that we got the chance to commit our whole lives and essences to the cause. That's what the last battle was for me. It was a culmination of my commitment to Truydan. I was going to die, or I was going to die trying. There was no other option, and I wouldn't have chosen otherwise.

Of course, I'm here now, telling this story. I didn't die.

My commitment didn't end. My cause has been reduced to ashes. Everything, *everyone*, is ashes except the few of us who managed to find our way off the surface. Our promise to Truydan still stands, even though we're probably the only Truydanis left to ever know if that promise was fulfilled.

The abominations must die. They're not human.

I still remember the sound of those words, as stated by my instructor during the extensive training I received in preparation for my service to the great state of Truydan. They flashed through my mind as I ran up the tower stairs. I knew I should be afraid. It was a one-way trip. But I wasn't afraid. I was vindicated. I was ready to die.

I wasn't even winded when I reached the top of the flight. It was easy to dispatch the two security guards perched at the doorway. They were the same kind of monstrosities I'd been seeing since I arrived at Chancellor City some weeks prior. Leggy, augmented things with stretched-out, pale faces and way too much hair in all the wrong spots. The reach of their claws was impressive, and their grip strength was beyond deadly.

But even with their surgical enhancements and bio-integrated Arachnotech, they were disappointing opponents. They all moved the same, used the same techniques, and made the same sounds when they died. They all even bled the same exact dirty maroon. I know because I killed thirteen of them by the time I reached the Chancellor's chambers.

I glanced around, then pressed my palm to the massive door, preparing myself for what I knew would be the most hideous sight I would ever see in my life. Then, silent as a cat in my special-issue suit, I cracked the door and slipped in, laser-blade in hand and ready.

Inside was dark, which was unsurprising. The

Arachnids and their mutant pets love to live in the darkest, dankest corners. My visor lit up red and green, and I scanned the room for any signs of Arachnid life. But the strange thing was that, even with my tools, I couldn't see anything.

I was alone in the room.

Or I thought I was. Despite EMCON Alpha status, my radio lit up and gave away my position. There was a blinding pulse of light, and something came rushing at me. And then the floor dropped out beneath me, and I fell into a sea of roiling chaos.

I braced for impact, but instead of hitting the ground, I was tossed into the undertow and whipped around by the flow of brick and stone. I surfaced for a moment, then was pulled back under. It was what I imagine being chewed up might feel like – but all the teeth are too dull to do the job and finish you off, so you're just getting ground up and worn down piece by painful piece.

I don't know how long I was in it, but I do know it stopped because the next thing I knew, I was waking up beneath the brightest sky I had ever seen. Everywhere was the pale orange-gray of ash and smoke and spore, and the unholy brightness of the Arachno-cultists' mega-bomb descending on the earth like a second sun. I had heard they were going to drop it on us – I had hoped to have completed my mission before then.

There was a voice in my ear, faint and scattered. I had no idea what was being said, only that I could barely breathe enough to reply. And then, someone leaned over me. Their shadow blocked out the sun, and then I could feel them lifting me up. My bones screamed, my muscles felt like rubber bands holding splintered wood in place. It was too much, and everything went dark again.

And then I woke up inside Duff's drop pod. We were moving so unbelievably fast, faster than I had ever gone in a dinghy like that. The whole thing was shaking like it was going to break apart, and at first, I thought we had lost power and were plummeting toward earth. Then Bran was there, saying something.

"... but we can't take your helmet off. We need your suit to keep everything together. We're going to make it, right Duff?"

"I sure hope so." And then the shockwave hit, blasting us out even faster. The shuttle got even hotter and fishtailed. "Hold her down; I can't keep it steady!" Duff said, letting go of the stick and hitting some buttons on the dash. We slid quickly into a spiral, and Bran was over me, his arms and legs braced against the bench seats at the sides of the craft, cushioning the backboard I was strapped to.

"Don't worry," he said, "I won't throw up on you."

I wanted to laugh. I wanted to cry. Instead, I tried to breathe – a wet wheeze came out, spattering the inside of my helm with bright blood.

Bran's face went serious again as he fought to keep me steady. "You're going to make it, Avery." But I could see he was starting to lose consciousness. The rest of the crew, save Duff, had lost the battle a few moments before, but the ship's spin slowed as its corrective autopilot systems finally started to do their job.

Between flashes of blue-black space, I watched the Shatterer's fireball envelop the surface and atmosphere of the Earth. I knew then that we would never be able to return home again.

Redemption on the Horizon

Waking up from hyper-sleep is always rough on the body. Even supersoldiers struggle sometimes. They were the last to lay down for the long sleep and the first to wake up. Avery opens her eyes, greeted by the painful bright white of the hypersleep bay. At first, she thinks she is back on Earth, reliving her own personal hell. The fear passes quickly, like a shiver down her spine. Slick with life-sustaining fluids, she pulls herself out of the hyperchamber. Still naked, she makes her way between the rows of sleep pods toward the showers.

Duff and Bran wake up in neighboring pods a few rows away. Bran is the first thing Duff sees when he opens his eyes.

"Good morning, sleeping beauty," Bran says.

Duff grins, sitting up and bracing himself against the spin of the room as his body and mind orient themselves in space and time. "It always feels just like a blink to me."

Bran stretches, bioenhanced muscles rippling against his scarred skin. "Well I feel rested. Even got some dreaming in!" He helps Duff out of the hyper-sleep chamber and the two walk toward the showers.

"Lucky, I never dream in those things."

"Eh, it doesn't happen for everyone."

Duff pauses, looking out the bay window at the large red planet looming in the distance. "Are we sure they're there?"

"Last I heard, that's what the intel said," Bran replies, throwing a fresh towel at his friend. "Come on, before the hot water's gone."

Steam wafts out of the shower room as super soldiers walk single file through the spray of almost-too-hot water and soap. Rinse, suds, rinse, dry. On the other side, they're presented with a set of gray travel sweats and a data slate with information about the mission at hand. It almost feels like old times. Almost.

"Guys!" Avery calls from the far end of the room, by the exit. "Hurry up; I'm starving!" They push through the growing mass of super-soldiers and meet her in the corridor, dressing as they walk.

"So what does it say?" Bran asks, eyeing what looks like the exact same mess meal they had the day they went into the hyper-pods.

"I don't know, I haven't looked yet," Duff replies, tossing two solid hunks of protein substitute onto his tray.

"It says there's a place near a crater on the north side. That's where they think the colony is," Avery says, piling more food onto her tray.

"A whole colony?" Duff asks.

"That's what the report said. We'll be in position in just a few weeks, so you'll need to train up extra hard to get ready."

"I have no problem besting you in the training cages again," Bran says, a smile playing at his lips. Avery throws a piece of her carboloaf at him, and it hits his forehead.

But Duff remains serious, and they all sit down at the table by the exit. "What's at the colony? Is it a military installation?"

"Looks like a research facility of some kind. Scouts said they found some tech there that might be worth salvaging." Avery points to his data slate, and it lights up, displaying a map of the expected enemy territory on Mars. "You could try reading the brief for yourself, you know."

Duff swallows a bite of food and nods, glancing down at the slate. "But is it full of spider-people?"

Avery shrugs, "I assume so, since they're the ones we're after."

Bran shudders. "They're so creepy."

"They're not just creepy, they're dangerous, remember?" Avery chides him. "Duff is right, this is serious and we need to start planning now."

Bran throws a glare at Avery from across the table. "I know. I was there, too. I'm just trying to have a little fun before we have to get all serious..."

"I don't understand," Duff says, ignoring the pissing match between his friends, "If they escaped to mars, *all* of them –"

" – most of them –" Avery interjects.

"--*Most* of them, how could they fit in such a small region?"

"Well, they're probably underground, like how they lived on Earth? You know, in hives," Bran says.

"Fuck." Duff says, sucking on a particularly sweet, stringy piece of the reconstituted vegetable product. "Do you think that whole thing is full of them?"

"If they found a way to multiply without converting new humans, then maybe. It depends on how quickly and effectively they can reproduce," Avery theorizes. "But that's not really our concern. We're here to wipe them out however we can."

"It's a suicide mission," Bran says, like it was obvious even before they had a mission report to refer to.

Avery had always planned to die for Truydan, and Bran only ever wanted to live or die fighting side by side with his comrades. But Duff had had plans. He and Jindra were supposed to make it out alive, retire, build a life outside the blood and gore.

"I guess you're right," Duff says, accepting that none of

his life-long dreams could ever come true. They couldn't, not with Jindra, with the whole world obliterated from existence. There could only ever be this, the final act of revenge – of redemption. There could only ever be their plan to descend on the scourge that had taken their lives and livelihoods from them.

After a pause, Avery asks, "But what if it's not?" Her voice is tight. Something unknowable, forbidden strains the strings of her vocal cords.

"Then we find wherever the rest of them are hiding, and we wipe them out, too," Duff says.

"And we keep going until every last one of the bastards is dead, and there are a hundred of them killed for every one of our brothers they murdered," Bran finishes.

Avery smiled, and they all reached out and held each other's hands. "Then we better get ready. We make planetfall in seventeen days."

9

RED DUST CHILD

JB LETTERCAST WITH MARÍA G. ORELLANA

...

BEEP.

BEEP.

BEEP.

Will that sound ever stop?

BEEP.

BEEP.

BEEEEEEEEEEEP!

Blinking. I'm blinking. It's bright. It hurts. My eyes are open, but all I see is blurred nothingness. I will them closed with a struggle, sticky eyelids fighting me. It's almost just as bright when they're closed. My head swims and pulses. I might be sick. No, I won't be sick. I refuse to throw up again.

Again?

I don't remember throwing up before, but I must have. There is the familiar cool of metal on my back. How long have I been here? Where even is *here?* I breathe, grounding myself in my body before sitting up. I feel like I'm on a boat. I squint my eyes open, hoping to quell the seasickness.

Tunnel vision spirals as the room's edges come very slowly and painfully into focus. I try to look down at my body, but the pain in my neck is too much. I really can't turn my head without turning my whole body. The tunnel vision lingers, even as the oceanic swaying within me becomes tolerable, and I begin to piece together exactly where I am.

The room is clinical, sterile, white. A fluorescent light flickers above a row of painfully bright computer screens. It seems one of these computers is the source of the incessant beeping that woke me up in the first place. There are piles of paper stacked messily across the computer desk. Carefully, I stand and make my way to try and read what I can.

But the stacked papers are written in some kind of language I can't read. Or maybe I can't read at all. Letters look like jumbled lines, and nothing seems to make any kind of sense. Even graphs, where numbers and math would have given me a clue, seem completely nonsensical.

The first monitor, the beeping one, displays a series of what appear to be vital signs, but everything is written in that same, confusing language. I notice the wires stuck to my chest and temples, and pull them off painfully in an effort to make the beeping stop. As the connections are severed, the beeping turns into an eerie wail. Well, fuck.

I move on to the next monitor. It's a black screen that occasionally flashes red. At the center, in big letters, read the words

> *CRITICAL ERROR. ALL PROCESSES TERMINATED. SYSTEM SUSPENDED.*

The sinking feeling in my chest tells me something is

terribly, horribly wrong. Well, at least I know I can read something. This one must be in a language I know.

The final monitor is a massive one. It takes up about one quarter of the wall, and the screen is divided up into about twenty smaller screens, some blank, some depicting strange, abstract-art-looking images. A tangle of cords hook up to the monitor, connecting it to a collection of microscopes on another desk along the adjacent wall. Many of them are knocked over, samples spilled all over the floor. Above that desk is what appears to be a window into the next room.

I step closer. Maybe if I can look at the samples, or glance out the window there, I'll know something about why I'm here. I try to pick my way through the broken glass on the floor, but the tunnel vision makes it hard. A stab of pain shoots up through my foot as the *click* of glass breaking echoes loudly through the room. When I try to bend over and look at my foot, I find that I can't. The pain in my back is too much. I swallow hard against the burn of acid in my throat, and move on to the other side of the room. The sting of glass in my foot mixes in with the noise of the rest of the pain inhabiting my body.

The wall across the computer monitors is plastered with shards of broken ceramic and stained with spatters of drying coffee. A keyboard letter, "T," is lodged in the wall like a throwing star. The rest of its family are littered at the base of the wall, scattered across a graveyard of broken keyboards, shredded wires, and coffee mugs. A titanium medical bracelet gleams in the fluorescent light. It's speckled with what could be coffee, or syrup, or something else. I would pick it up if I could bend over far enough to reach it.

Confusion gives way to fear, and I want to cry. I want to

yell. I want *anything* but whatever this is. Something bad happened here – might still be happening – and I have no idea who or where I am. I need to find answers. I need to find a way out. I need both of these things *fast*.

One look around tells me that if I'm alone, it's recent. There had to have been people here with me. Working on me, maybe? I glance back at the enormous medical table at the center of the room. A shudder passes through me as images flash through my mind. Lab coats. Blue masks. Purple nitrile gloves. The stench of antiseptic. The sting of lidocaine. The taste of saline at the back of my throat.

But why?

I go to the door on the far wall. It's closed, maybe even locked. But I don't even have to touch the handle because as I approach, it slides open with a gentle chime. There is a rush of cool air as I step out into the cadet-grey hallway. The door slides shut behind me, and the beeping finally subsides behind the soundproofed operating room walls.

I turn around to face the door, and it does not open again, no matter how close I get to it. Above it is a sign that reads

> *DR. ALYSSIA FERESHOVA, ASSISTANT HISTOPATHOLOGIST*

I reach above the door, fingers brushing the brownish-red grime off the sign as I slide it from its holster on the wall. The name means nothing to me, but it's a clue.

The grim hallway doesn't make me feel any better than the painfully white room did. The light is less harsh here, with only a few can lights flickering above the center of the hallway. Electric sparks fall to the floor, illuminated by flashing red lights that bring the roiling ocean inside me to the fore. Aerator vents hiss like crashing waves as I pass by beneath them. Recycled air washes over me, cool and dry. I smell iron. It's familiar.

It's uncannily hot under the vents that don't work, and claustrophobia nips at my heels as I make my way down the narrow corridor. It worsens as I weave my way through a tangled mess of exposed wires that hang like a knot of spaghetti from the torn-up ceiling there. I can't stop the feeling that something is watching me from the dark void above, or that I'll be sucked out through the opening there and shot off into... where? Space?

I try knocking on the few doors I see in this hallway, but no one answers. The doors don't open, either. I try typing random numbers into keypads at rooms with names above the doors, but am met with a disgruntled, monotone trill each time I fail. The thick smell of iron and decay seeps from the gaps beneath some of the doors. I don't want to think about what that might mean.

Eventually, I make it to the end of the hallway. I am met with frigid cold blasting from the vents as I round the corner. The red lights flash more brightly here, with absolutely no light coming from the ceiling to soften them. In the moments between flashes, amidst what I know should be pitch black, I can actually see. But the bright halo of the red lights leaves imprints on my vision, disorienting me to the point that I'm effectively as blind as I was when I first woke up.

I take a few steps forward, then find myself running as something crashes loudly behind me. I run, trip, catch myself, and turn around to face whatever it might have been, only to find that one of the ceiling beams had given way. My way back is officially blocked off by rubble, rebar, and live wires.

Is there something happening on the second floor? Or is the ceiling just unstable? Is that why I was left here to die? Was the place evacuated and I just didn't wake up soon enough from whatever procedure they were doing on me? Any good doctor would have brought their patient with them during an evacuation. Maybe there was an earthquake and there just wasn't time to drag me out with them.

I continue forward, and moments later I reach a door that is half-heartedly sliding open and shut. It's stuck on something on the floor, something that looks like a person's leg in tweed pants and a rubber boot. Just the leg, nothing else. I must be in shock because all I can think about is how silly a random leg would be in an entirely empty medical facility like this. Laughter streams out of me, like it's the funniest joke I've ever heard.

I hope I'm dreaming.

There is the *drip, drip, drip* of liquid hitting the floor beneath me, then the sizzle of acid eating the floor. Must be a leak from the ceiling. A glance up shows no sign of an exposed pipe, and I hope that whatever is falling from the ceiling does not land on me. Heat rushes through me as I jump forward, prying the door open long enough to get myself through it. I leave the leg where it is, in case I need to come back this way.

Another white room, but this one is massive and uncomfortably warm. The words

> *VIVARIUM, AREA 0*

are painted in large orange letters that dominate the far

wall. The air is stale with the stench of formaldehyde and other indistinguishable but equally abhorrent chemicals. Rows of large glass tanks line all sides of the octagonal room, at the center of which is another medical slab and desk set-up.

The tanks are filled with microecosystems. All manner of colors fill my senses, to the point of overwhelm. I can smell and taste every living thing – every *dying* thing – in this room. And yes, the plants and creatures living within the glass domes are all dying.

As I get closer to the center of the room, the heat intensifies. I know somewhere in the back of my brain that it's too warm for these delicate microclimates to thrive without some kind of climate control operating to maintain the temperature and humidity within each of the tanks.

One glance at the computers at the center of the room tells me the climate control systems are not online. Of course, the nauseating perfume of warm decay that filled the room was enough to tell me nothing here will survive the apparently failed air vents and downed computer systems. I feel grief rear its ugly head in my chest at the loss of all the time and effort spent to maintain these microecosystems, and the lives inside them.

I rifle through the papers on the desk, all proving as nonsensical as those I tried to read in the operating room. I look at the walls, doors, and equipment for any kind of map or key card I can use to try and access the other parts of the facility, to no avail. Everything, even the warnings on the different complicated machines and tubes and tanks, is written in that same language that I feel like I know, but just can't seem to grasp.

On one of my rounds, I come across a particularly

strong, acrid stench. I follow the smell to a crystalline sarcophagus, which is much larger than the others, toward the entrance to the room, and inside is the paper-skinned form of a human being. Indigo veins bulge against fragile, yellow skin as they float in a tank of viscous, translucent blue fluid.

Their face is malformed, large mouth pulled wide in a painful, rectangular gape. Sharp teeth, and something else I can't quite make out, force it into its unnatural rectangular shape. The eyelids are sewn shut, scars not yet formed over dissolvable stitches. A piece of eyeball rebels against the sutures on the right eye, forcing itself, gray and puffy, through a gap in the hasty stitch-work.

It's uncanny but not nearly as disturbing as the arms, which fade from yellow to gray to bone-white starting at the elbow. The fingers are long, forming at the base of what must have been the human's natural wrist, and extending down to their toes.

And the fingers are not individual digits, stretching instead into a single point, emphasized by a shard of what must be cartilage or bone. It's growing to cover the majority of the hands and arms, clearly making its way upward toward the shoulders. Some of it can be seen growing on the human's soles, too, like shoes, up the calves and around to the shins like armor. All along the stark white of the cartilage is small dark hairs, like very coarse fur, that undulates gently in the quasi-currents of the tank.

This is no human. Maybe it had been at one time, but now it's some poor victim of science gone wrong. I think it's dead. I hope it is. But I can't be certain. The stench that led me to it has mixed in with the rest of the overwhelming stink of this room, and now I'm not so sure this particular creature is what stank so bad in the first place.

There's no way to tell if the bubbles I just saw escape from its nose are remnants of a life past. There's no way to know for certain if the slight twitch of its head is a result of the tank cycling its fluids, or if it was the stirrings of a creature that has realized it's being watched.

I feel the urge to run. I listen, even as the bile rises in my throat, and find an open corridor with a set of stairs. I take the exit, reaching another door that opens without prompting. I wish I had a leg to stuff into it, to keep it from locking me out of what might be my only escape as I work my way deeper into this unending labyrinth, but the door slides shut before I can think to stuff something in between it and the doorframe.

I turn with a sigh to see another long corridor, this one well-lit and lined with doors on both sides. Must be a housing section. The air is working here, thrusting me into unbearable dryness and bleak chill. My headache returns with a dizzying rush. I hadn't even realized it had gone, and I want to turn back to the humid hotness of the vivarium. But the door remains closed when I approach it, so I move on.

I try most of the doors lining the hallway, to no avail. These ones do not smell of iron and decay, which gives me hope that maybe someone might be living up here. But as I round a corner into a much darker corridor, I see that my path is blocked by a beam and its accompanying rubble, which I presume to be the same piece of ceiling that came crashing down behind me before I reached the vivarium.

Electricity flickers as I approach. After a brief assessment, I decide that it might as well be impossible to pick my way through the wreckage and make it to the other side of the hallway, and I can't go back because the door is closed. Can I climb up to the next floor? I move to grip the main beam, expecting to struggle against the slick surface, or to cut my hands on the metal, or strain my back as I scramble up.

Instead, I make my way up with ease.

Poking my head up to the next floor, I see a wider hallway, at the end of which is a set of double doors labeled

> *CONFERENCE ROOM*

It's seconds before I'm standing in front of the doors. As I move to try and open them, a door in my periphery slides open. I glance at the dark room presenting itself to me. Is it a trap? Unable to resist the haunting allure of it, I step inside.

Humid. Quiet. I hadn't realized the hum of electricity was so pervasive in the rest of the facility until now. My eyes don't take long to adjust. It smells earthy here, like the wet soil of a forest floor, like cool leaves in the summer sun, like desert sage after a heavy rain. A light mist hovers above the ground and at eye level. And then I see them.

Just barely illuminated by some internal light source are small, delicate, brown and purple orbs, seated in what appear to be clusters of six and seven. The bioluminescence of, what I can only assume are *eggs*, is interrupted by the trembling of small, purplish things moving around on the inside. I look closer, hesitant but also feeling somewhat responsible to these unknown, unborn creatures, and see that a few of the eggs have begun to soften in preparation for hatching.

I want to stay and watch. I want to see them take their first breaths, whatever they are. I feel a kinship with them. Maybe I was their caretaker, before I completely lost all memory of who I am. I wonder if I was a part of whatever experiments were going on with that post-human creature in the large tank at the vivarium.

The sweet-iron-smell of blood draws my attention away from my musing. Could there possibly be someone else here? Eyes adjusted fully to the dark, I manage to follow fresh, bloody drag marks out of the egg-room, toward the conference room with the double doors. I make a note of where the eggs are, and decide to return as soon as I make sure whoever is bleeding is either okay, or too far gone to help.

And if they're alive, maybe they can tell me what the hell is going on around here. If they're not...

The *drip, drip, drip* of another leaking pipe, and the *hissssss* of acid just barely misses my head again, pooling on the floor beneath my chin, just out of sight.

The smell of blood gets much stronger as I pass over the threshold into the conference room. It's stark blue in here, uncomfortably blue, like dead computer blue. The wall to my right sports a bay window, looking out across red-brown sand and a pink sky, littered with dirt devils and the pinprick of the sun as it nears the horizon. *Mars.*

I know where I am! Well, sort of. I know this room. Despite the disheveled nature of the place, I have the familiar sense that I spent many hours in this room on a weekly. Chairs are strewn about the room, some splintered to toothpicks, some suspended from the ceiling in silk web. The oblong conference table I know I've sat at for boring meetings and stressful planning committees, is broken in half.

Once again, can lights flicker anxiously and red lights flash at the head and base of the only exit, which is the double doors I just passed through. The bouquet of death punches at my sinuses. Rotting flesh. Despite the dizziness that sends me reeling, I maintain enough composure to count almost thirty bodies. Bodies, broken like the chairs, bound in inhuman positions by that unmistakable sticky silk web. *Arachnids.*

Some blood pools on the floor, but most of them seem completely drained. Some of them are headless, or missing other parts. Some of them are just torsos, just legs, some flayed in half so their entrails dangle out like corporate birthday party decorations. Some are still breathing, stored, like leftovers, to be eaten or evacuated of their warm life-force, then served up as putrefaction to the beetles and maggots and probably to whatever was about to hatch in the next room over.

My mind shatters as the screams of the dying fill me. Pity, empathy, terror, guilt, shame, all course through me and the sorrow of it all drags me closer to the corpses. Upon closer inspection, most of the deceased sport unsightly, oozing growths, and calcification on parts of their skin. Patches of long, coarse, brown hairs grow in patches along some of the calcified skin. Those that still have eyes seem to be growing extra pairs. Mouths that I previously perceived as simply gaped in horror are actually spread open by uncomfortable-looking dental mutations.

How terrifying it must have been for them to suffer such an unfortunate fate. I can't recognize a single one of them, be it from amnesia or the sheer magnitude of their malformities in death, but I know that not one of them deserved this sort of fate.

I find dog tags on some of the corpses, others scattered around the floor. One tagless body at the far left of the room calls to me. The face is gone. There is just a thick flap of skin drooping from the neck, with evidence of a chin and the trace of what might have been lips. The lips flash through my mind as a series of memories. Kissing. Gentleness. Skin on skin. Hands caressing hands in the humid dark of the egg-room as she whispers promises of a bright new future between euphoric sighs. *Dr. Fereshova.*

Alyssia.

Grief hits me again. I want to weep. I want to scream. I find that I cannot. I can only reach rage, and for a moment, I think to tear the web down and burn all the bodies, to stop their unceremonious decay in this ugly blue conference room. But I don't. Touching the web could likely wind me up with the same fate as them, and I refuse to die here.

As I contemplate my next move, my eye catches something moving behind the ghastly display of corpses arranged around Alyssia's headless body. I squint and lean in, and hungry, violet eyes stare back. My stomach drops, my knees feel weak, and I freeze.

The beast staring back at me stays crouched, unblinking, watching to see if I will make its next kill difficult by running, or easy by staying put. After a few seconds, I wonder if it's seen me at all. Maybe it's sleeping with its eyes open. Maybe it's dead. Either way, I know for certain this is the Arachnid that made this web. It's likely the mother to the eggs in the next room over.

I don't take long to make my decision. I'm not going to die here. I move to run, juking left then diving right toward the conference table. The beast follows me exactly, seemingly already aware of my plan. But I catch a glimpse of something as I drop painfully to the floor.

Was that a patch of paper-thin skin? Could the beast possibly be some post-human concoction, like the one in the tank at the vivarium? Can I reason with it?

Slowly, I stand.

It mimics me, peering between strands of web. It's hungry and savage and coated in viscera.

I hold my hands up, trying to steady it with a human gesture of peace. It follows suit, long spindly spires of bone protruding from its elbows and ending in sharp points where fingers should be. I take a slow step forward, and it does the same.

And then it dawns on me. All the years of meetings in this stupid blue room, I always made sure I sat across from the mirror so I could watch Alyssia's sarcastic expressions as our project director trilled on about budgets and bottom lines.

The mirror.

Which is partly hidden by webs and dead bodies.

The mirror.

Which I am facing, right now.

The baleful eyes, enormous and bulging, of which there are six – no, eight, but two have been carved completely out and two more are seeping yellow-green pus – are mine. The ghastly chelicerae stretching my face in an uncanny grin, acid saliva dripping from their fangs, are all mine. The arms, long and spindly, the disjointed legs, the pumping, bulging thorax, all coated in wiggling brown hairs – all of this is *me*.

Only two parts of this nightmarish likeness do not belong to me. First, the sprays of coagulating blood that coat my fur, which undoubtedly came from my murdered colleages. Second, the remainder of Alyssia's face, which dangles like a bad Halloween mask from my right fang.

As I lean in closer to observe, mortified and fascinated, disgusted and intrigued, I hear the sound of gunfire outside. The sun is dropping below the horizon, and the night sky is littered with the yellow and red fire-streaks of drop pods entering the atmosphere. Glimmering red puffs of dust fly high into the atmosphere as metal-clad soldiers and their vehicles approach.

I can only imagine what new horrors await me in this waking nightmare.

Drip, drip, drip.

Hisssssss.